BABY, IT'S COLD OUTSIDE

A RESCUE MY HEART NOVEL

KAIT NOLAN

Baby, It's Cold Outside

2nd Edition

Written and published by Kait Nolan

Cover design by Kait Nolan

Copyright 2019 Kait Nolan

Original Copyright 2018 Kait Nolan

AUTHOR'S NOTE: The following is a work of fiction. All people, places, and events are purely products of the author's imagination. Any resemblance to actual people, places, or events is entirely coincidental.

A LETTER TO READERS

Dear Reader,

This book is set in the Deep South. As such, it contains a great deal of colorful, colloquial, and occasionally grammatically incorrect language. This is a deliberate choice on my part as an author to most accurately represent the region where I have lived my entire life. This book also contains swearing and pre-marital sex between the lead couple, as those things are part of the realistic lives of characters of this generation, and of many of my readers.

If any of these things are not your cup of tea, please consider that you may not be the right audience for this book. There are scores of other books out there that are written with you in mind. In fact, I've got a list of some of my favorite authors who write on the sweeter side on my website at https://kaitnolan.com/on-the-sweeter-side/

If you choose to stick with me, I hope you enjoy!

Happy reading!

Kait

CHAPTER 1

"**W**here are your pages, Ivy?"

Ivy Blake winced at the snap of her agent's voice on the other end of the phone. Marianne was pulling out her stern, mom-of-three tone. That was never good. "They're coming."

At some theoretical, future time that was actually true.

"You've been saying that for weeks. And you've been avoiding me. You only do that when the words aren't flowing."

You have no idea.

"The book's been giving me a smidge of trouble." Understatement of the century. "But I promise, I'm nearly done." Flagrant lie. Ivy wondered if Marianne's Momdar was sounding an alarm. Ivy's own mama had an Eyebrow of Doom that could be heard over the phone when engaged.

"You have to give me something to give to Wally. I can't hold him off much longer."

Walter Caine—who inexplicably went by Wally, a fact that made it utterly impossible to take him seriously—was currently at the top of Ivy's avoid-at-all-costs list. Her editor was brilliant but a bit like a banty rooster when he got angry. He had deadlines. Of course, Ivy understood that. Everything about publishing involved deadlines. He'd absolutely blow a gasket if he knew she was still on Chapter One. The thirteenth version.

It was probably a sign.

"Next week." Was this what it felt like to be in debt to a bookie? Making absurd promises in hopes of avoiding broken kneecaps or cement shoes? Except in this case it was Ivy's career, not her actual life, in danger.

"Ivy." Marianne drew her name out to four syllables, which was tantamount to being middle-named by her mama.

Ivy hunched her shoulders. "I swear I'm finishing up the book. In fact, I'm taking a special trip for the express purpose of focusing on nothing but that until it's done."

Where the hell had that come from? She had no such plans. Apparently in lieu of offering up reasonable plot, her brain had decided to just spew spontaneous, bald-faced lies.

Her agent sighed. "Fine. How can I reach you?"

In for a penny...

"Oh, well, you can't. There's no internet up there, and I was warned that cell service is spotty. The cabin has absolute privacy and no distractions. It's perfect."

Actually, something like that *did* sound perfect. If she went totally off the grid, Marianne and Wally wouldn't know where to send the hitman when she missed her deadline. The one that had already been pushed back once.

You've never missed a final deadline, and you're not going to start now.

Marianne offered another beleaguered sigh. "Find an internet connection and check in on Monday or I'm hunting you down, understand?"

"Yes, ma'am." Ivy had no doubt she meant it. Despite her trio of children and the stable of other writers she managed, Marianne would absolutely get herself on a plane and show up on Ivy's doorstep if she thought it would get results.

"I'll do what I can to hold off Wally. This morning's starred review at Kirkus for *Hollow Point Ridge* should appease him for a little while. You know he loves nothing more than seeing you rack up acclaim."

"Because acclaim means dollar signs for us all," Ivy recited. As if she could forget that it was more than just her depending on income from her books.

"Damn straight. I forwarded the review to you. Check your email before you go," Marianne ordered.

She'd already seen the review this morning. Somebody had posted it in her fan group, which had generated a discussion thread that was already twenty pages deep about where she planned to go with the series next. But bringing that up would only prolong this conversation.

"Will do."

"Happy writing."

For just a moment, Ivy considered coming clean and telling Marianne the stark, unvarnished truth. Her agent was, ultimately, meant to be her advocate. But right now, she was only more pressure. So Ivy held in her snort of derision as she hung up the phone and tossed it on her desk.

It had been a long damned time since she'd been happy writing. The truth was, she had a raging case of writer's block, and she was already weeks past her initial deadline. That wasn't like her at all. She was a machine. Her first three books had poured out of her. The next three were each successively bigger, deeper, harder. And with each had come more success and higher expectations from her publisher, who wanted to capitalize on momentum to maximize sales. That was a business decision on their part. She was a commodity. Ivy understood that. And up to now, she'd been able to work with it.

But along with the professional pressures had come the rabid excitement of her fans. They loved the world she created, the characters she'd given them, and not a day went by when she didn't get emails and messages on social media demanding to know when the next book was coming because OMG they needed it yesterday! They had no idea the months, sometimes years of work that went into each book. What ate up her entire life occupied theirs for mere hours or days. And their insatiable enthusiasm was just one more stone piling on and crushing her with stress.

This book wasn't like the other six in her best-selling series, and she just hadn't found the right hook yet.

She would. Of course, she would. She just needed some more time and less pressure.

"Why don't you ask for world peace, while you're at it?"

Dropping into her office chair, Ivy shoved back from the desk and rolled across her office to the massive whiteboard occupying one wall. At this stage, the whole surface should've been covered with color-coded sticky notes detailing the assorted character arcs and how they drove and were driven by the action of the external plot. But it was empty other than the scrawl of "Michael" at the top in red marker. Below it a bright yellow note read, *You are a stubborn, taciturn asshole, who won't talk to me.* In a fit of pique and stress cleaning earlier in the week, she'd stripped away version number twelve of her plot. Now she couldn't face the blank space.

Page fright was so much a real thing.

Maybe she *should* get away. Find one of those out-of-the-way cabins to rent, with no phone, no internet, no way to be crushed under the weight of other people's expectations. Maybe then she could hear herself think.

Rolling back to her computer, she opened a browser, compulsively clicking on the little envelope that told her she had seventy-nine unread messages.

She'd cleared her inbox this morning.

"Why do I do this to myself?"

She started to close it out when a subject line caught her attention.

Come visit the brand new spa at The Misfit Inn!

She'd forgotten about The Misfit Inn. Last summer, she and several girlfriends had taken a weekend trip up there in spontaneous celebration of Deanna's divorce. The owners had mentioned they were considering adding a spa. Ivy had signed up for the mailing list and promptly forgotten about it. She opened the email, feeling the first hints of excitement as she read it. Okay, maybe that was desperation. But really? A spa? One set right in the gorgeous Smoky Mountains, just four short hours away? She desperately needed to relax. It had to be a sign from the Universe.

Someone answered on the second ring. "Thank you for calling The Misfit Inn. This is Pru. How can I help you?"

Ivy remembered Pru, the kind-hearted woman who'd done everything possible to make the inn feel like home.

"This is Ivy Blake. I don't know if you remember me, but a bunch of girlfriends and I stayed with y'all last summer for a Thank God I'm Divorced party weekend—"

"Deanna's group! Yes, certainly we remember y'all."

"Well, I got the email about the opening of the spa, and it did say call to ask about booking specials that covered the inn and spa, so here I am."

"Wonderful!" The genuine warmth in Pru's voice had some of the knots relaxing. "How many?"

"Just me."

"In need of some pampering?"

"You have no idea."

"Okay then. When were you wanting to come?"

The sooner the better. "Um...today?"

"Today! Good gracious. Y'all are all about the spontaneity aren't you?"

Sure, let's call it that. "I know it's last-minute, but I was hoping to book two weeks."

"We can certainly accommodate that. But you should know before you make the drive that we're supposed to be having some really serious winter weather. Full-on snow and ice. The drive is liable to be pretty nasty and there's a really good chance you could get snowed in."

Snowed in at an inn and spa for two weeks, far away from everyone who knew her? "That sounds absolutely perfect. I'll see you in a few hours."

~

GRIEF SMELLED OF ONIONS, cheese, and cream of something soup. Multiple tables groaned under the weight of death casseroles along one wall of the church fellowship hall. The scent of it wafted over as Harrison Wilkes walked in, simultaneously curdling his stomach and making it growl. A quick scan of the room told him the widow hadn't made it over from the cemetery yet, but he spotted the man he'd come to support hovering near the dessert table. Careful not to make eye contact with the other mourners, Harrison wove his way through the crowd.

If possible, Ty looked worse than he had during the service. But then, he was here against medical advice and had served as a pall bearer. Sweat beaded along his brow. His shoulder had to be hurting like a son of a bitch from over-exertion.

"Sit your ass down before you fall down, Brooks."

Ty lifted bloodshot eyes to Harrison's. "You're not my CO."

"I'm still your friend." He took a step closer and lowered his voice. "You did your duty to Garrett. Don't you go blowing all the work you've done in PT by pushing yourself too far."

Ty's pale face turned mulish, but before he could pop off, another familiar voice interrupted.

"Step aside, y'all. I've got food to add to the table."

Sebastian Donnelly muscled his way past, a casserole dish in hand. Its contents smelled both familiar and noxious.

"Tell me that's not what I think it is," Harrison said.

Sebastian plunked the dish down on the table and took off the foil. "My famous barbeque beef casserole."

"More like infamous," Ty said. "Only you would try to make a casserole out of MREs."

"I tried to talk him out of it." Porter Ingram joined the group. "We all know how much Garrett hated that shit."

Sebastian straightened, suddenly sober. "Yeah, but he'd hate this damned wake even more."

They all lapsed into silence, aware of the dubious privilege of standing here able to bitch and moan about the wake. A privilege Garrett didn't have.

Everything about this sucked. Funerals sucked to begin with, no matter who they were for. They sucked worse when it was a friend. Someone you'd fought alongside, who'd saved your ass, who should've made it home. And they sucked most when they brought up old shit you were still trying to move past. There were too many ghosts stirred up for anybody to be comfortable.

"Come on. Let's either make plates or go sit down." Porter's voice interrupted Harrison's thoughts.

"I'm not hungry," Ty insisted.

"Then let's get out of the way for the people who are." Porter smoothly managed to nudge him toward a table.

"Always the peacemaker," Harrison murmured.

"Yeah, he's good at that." Sebastian picked up a paper plate and began filling it from the assortment of dishes, skipping his own offering to the spread.

Not knowing what else to do, Harrison fell in behind him.

"How are you doing with all this?" Sebastian asked.

It was instinct to deflect. "Better than Ty."

They both looked across the room, where he'd finally sat, shoulders bowed, head bent as if he couldn't hold it up anymore. Porter had a chair pulled up, talking to him in a low voice, one hand on his arm.

Sebastian scooped up some kind of hash brown casserole. "You think he'll come back from this?"

"You never come back from this. Not really." Harrison twitched his shoulders inside the jacket of his suit, wishing the thing didn't feel like a straitjacket.

Glancing at Ty, seeing the clench of his jaw, the lines of strain fanning out from his eyes, Harrison knew exactly the kind of shit going through his buddy's head. He'd been there. It was the reason he'd left the Army. It didn't feel like three years. Not when so many familiar faces filled the room. Men he'd fought with, bled with. Many were still fighting the fight. In his own way, so was he. But he couldn't do what they did. Not anymore.

Harrison trailed Sebastian across the room, nodding acknowledgments to those who greeted him, but not stopping until he reached Ty's table. Ty went silent, straightening in his chair with a Styrofoam cup he no doubt wished held something stronger than sweet tea, as they all realized Bethany Reeves had just arrived.

Ty hadn't spoken to her at the funeral. He hadn't even been able to go near her. He blamed himself for Garrett's death. Wrongly. But none of them could talk him out of that at this stage. So the three of them ranged around him, buffers between their friend and everybody else here. They shoveled in food and talked football and other stupid, civilian shit because he needed distraction and it was all they could do here. But they each tracked Bethany's progress around the room and braced themselves when she made her way to Ty.

He didn't bolt. Ty was no coward and his mother had raised him better than that. But Harrison knew he wanted to.

Bethany's face was ravaged by grief as she reached out for Ty's hand. "Ty."

"Ma'am."

Her expression twisted. "Don't you ma'am me, Tyson Brooks. You were the closest thing Garrett had to a brother, and that makes you family."

Ty's Adam's apple bobbed. "I loved him like a brother."

"I know you did." She tried to smile, but tears streamed down her face. "He got out because of you. You're a hero for that."

Ty shoved to his feet so fast his chair tipped over, the metal clattering against the industrial tile floor as he jerked his hand from Bethany's. In the sudden silence, his words sounded too loud. "I'm no hero."

He walked out without another word. With apologetic looks at Bethany, Sebastian and Porter followed, no doubt to make sure he didn't do something stupid. That left Harrison to find the right thing to say to the poor woman to smooth things over. Fuck.

He didn't know how much Bethany knew about the details of her husband's death. Some of the details were classified, as Ranger missions often were. There were things he didn't know himself, but could easily fill in from experience. And he knew those things wouldn't bring comfort to Garrett's widow. In truth, he had no idea how to comfort those left behind. Standing beside her, looking into her stricken face, he felt all the old impotence rise up, strong enough to choke him.

Harrison didn't know what he said to Bethany. His head was too full of the visits he'd had to make to the significant others of his own men. But he said something, taking a moment to squeeze her hand because even he could tell she needed human connection. The grasp of her cold, clammy fingers sent him back, until his head echoed with tears and recriminations. Needing to get the hell out, he made his excuses and all but ran for the exit.

Outside the fellowship hall, he braced his hands against the trunk of a car and sucked in big, cleansing lungfuls of the cold, winter air. It was so cold it hurt, colder than it should be in north Georgia this time of year. But the pain was good. The pain brought him back to the now.

"Hey."

Harrison straightened and turned to Porter. "Where's Ty?"

"Sebastian took him home. He's gonna stick around a while, keep an eye on him."

"Good." Ty didn't need to be left alone right now. He had a long, dark road ahead.

Porter angled his head, studying Harrison with eyes that saw too much. "You're not looking so great."

Because it was Porter, because he'd see through the bullshit, Harrison admitted the truth. "I need to get the hell out of here."

"I've got a cabin nobody's using. It's a chunk out from town, away from everything and everybody. It's yours if you want it. Peace and quiet and a chance to get your head screwed on straight. And Eden's Ridge is closer than you driving all the way home."

The whole idea of being in the middle of nowhere in the mountains of Tennessee, away from people and pressures, where he could *think* was beyond appealing. He had some decisions to make. It would be easier to make them without all the reminders of the past.

"Lead the way."

CHAPTER 2

"They're going to ask Michael to come back," Ivy dictated into her phone app. "He's pissed about it because he quit the team for a reason. But they're going to ask, and he's trying to dodge the call."

Feeling an unexpected kinship with her recalcitrant hero, Ivy paused, fully aware of how much of herself she was putting into the story. After all, here she was driving four hours into the mountains, straight into an actual snowstorm, to avoid more calls from her own powers that be.

"So what extremes is he willing to go to in order to avoid these people? Somewhere remote. Rock climbing in the high desert. He's totally the type who'd be into that craziness. Maybe even climbing without safety gear because he's got that death-wish, guilt thing going on. And he gets to the top all in one piece, after some harrowing moment where he nearly fell to his death, and right as he's enjoying the peace, a helicopter shows up and...he realizes this is the opening scene to one of the *Mission Impossible* movies. Damn it."

Disgusted with herself, Ivy dug into the sack of road snacks she'd picked up at a gas station in the last town.

"Okay no high desert. Maybe he's going on some backwoods fishing expedition. In Alaska. Less people in Alaska, harder to get to. So he's on his way to...wherever he's going, and he stops for gas at some little hole-in-the wall place with two pumps and moose antlers over the door. He grabs some chips and some Twinkies. Because, why the hell not?"

She unwrapped one herself from the stash on the seat. "As he goes back out to the truck, he gets cornered by Annika. Because he's been under surveillance. Of course he has. And of course it's her. He could never run fast enough or far enough to get away from her. She was always in his thoughts. Sloan knew that, the bastard. So of course he'd send her to talk him into coming back to work."

Considering Annika's arguments, Ivy snarfed down one of the Twinkies. "So how does she convince him? What can she possibly say to make him change his mind? Is that a Twinkie, or are you just happy to see me?"

Ivy groaned and turned off the dictation. Comedic was not the tone for the series. But no amount of trying had helped her stay in the zone of serious. Also, she'd ruined Twinkies for herself. She couldn't sustain it because she just...didn't care if Michael agreed to come back to work. The man was tired. He deserved a damned break. Leave him alone with his fishing tackle and over-processed baked goods.

She took a huge bite out of a second snack cake.

Of course, Michael Keenan had a choice. Blake Iverson, aka Ivy Blake, was too busy eating Twinkies paid for with advance money for this book she hadn't written yet. And she was self-inserting into her plot way the hell too much. Probably inserting too much Hostess into herself, too.

She tossed the other half of the Twinkie back into the convenience store bag on the seat and put both hands on the wheel. Man, the snow was really starting to come down now.

As a girl raised in the Deep South, she wasn't used to this. The big, fat flakes made her feel like she was inside her Mawmaw Opal's prize snow globe. As a kid, Ivy used to shake it and stare for hours, praying for snow. Enough they'd get out of school and be able to build a snowman. Being within spitting distance of the Gulf Coast most of her life, it had never actually worked. But this —this was the real deal, and it was beautiful. Something she'd appreciate if she'd already made it to the inn and was standing inside it, beside a roaring fire with a mug of hot cocoa in hand. With marshmallows, because what was hot cocoa without marshmallows? But she was miles from the last town, and she was pretty sure she must have missed her turn while trying to navigate her missing plot.

Why hadn't she packed her GPS? Oh, right. Because she'd barely made it out with more than a suitcase of random clothes and her toothbrush before running with no plan other than getting the heck out of Dodge before Marianne flew in from Manhattan to personally check on her and the Book That Wasn't. Maybe she could pull the map up on her phone and figure out where the nearest sign of civilization was. She'd program in her destination and let her phone be navigator like a sane person.

"Siri, what is the nearest town?"

But the little iridescent blob on the screen never resolved into an answer. Not enough signal. Which meant there probably wasn't enough signal for Google Maps either.

Stealing a couple of quick glances from the road, she opened her music. The silence was getting to her. Stabbing the screen at random, she managed to kick off her Eighties Power Mix. Lifting her voice, Ivy joined Pat Benatar, wailing about love as a battle-field as she slowed for a switchback. By the time she'd rolled through some REO Speedwagon and on into Journey—was there any better band for road tripping?—she'd climbed to a higher elevation and the snow was coming down hard enough she actually heard it hit the windshield. Did that mean there was ice mixed in?

The more nervous she got, the louder she sang, until the windows all but rattled with her battle cry that she wouldn't stop believing. It was the best part of the song, and she lifted a hand off the wheel for a fist pump—just for a second.

The dark shape lumbered into the road.

Her high note turned into a scream as she hit the brakes. The Blazer fishtailed, the back end spinning to the front. Ivy wrestled the wheel, struggling to turn into the skid. She had a split second looking into the eyes of the bear before the SUV slammed into the guardrail, as if it were a stand of toothpicks, and went over the side.

"YOU SHOULD GET on the road, man. This storm is just gonna get worse."

Following Porter's gaze, Harrison looked out the window of Elvira's Tavern and had to agree. The thickening flakes had begun to coat the sidewalks of downtown Eden's Ridge. Tipping back the last of his drink, he shoved away from the table and offered his hand. "I really appreciate this."

Porter took his hand and pulled him in for a thumping hug. "Any time. And if you decide you wanna stay longer, you just say the word. The tourist rentals dry up to next to nothing this time of year, and I'm just as happy it's not sitting empty."

"Thanks. I'll let you know." At the rate he was going, he just might burrow in until spring. The real world held that little appeal.

"There's some stuff out there. Coffee, basic spices, some other non-perishables I keep on-hand for guests. But not enough to get you through the next few days if the weather turns like they're saying."

"I'll go by Garden of Eden before I get out of town."

"You need anything, you just holler. And that includes a friendly ear." Porter shot him a meaningful look.

He'd had a few years and more than a few offers of the same since he got out of the Army. But talking it out hadn't been his preferred form of processing the shit he brought back to civilian life. Not then and not now. "Understood. I'll give you a call on the flip side. Maybe we can get another beer and a pizza before I head back home."

Porter dipped his head in a nod. "That'd be good. Enjoy your quiet."

"It was good to see you, brother." And now, God willing, he wouldn't see another human being for the next six days.

After loading up on supplies, Harrison stopped, out of long-ingrained habit, to gas up the Jeep before he left town. Even in that little span of time, the snowfall seemed to have more than doubled. The cold front that had come through earlier in the week had primed the ground for actual accumulation, and it looked like they were gonna be in for a doozy.

The drive that, on a good day, should've taken a mere twenty minutes, stretched out near to an hour. Harrison practically crawled up the mountain in his Jeep. When he'd accepted Porter's offer to use his cabin for the week, he'd had no idea he'd need to put snow chains on. It was Tennessee for Chrissakes. It had been years since he'd driven in any real snow. At least while stateside and not driving a Hummer. The last thing he needed was to go sliding off the slick roads this far out from town.

On the radio, the song broke and the local DJ came on. "They're calling it Stormageddon, folks. It's getting ugly out there. Snow's coming thicker and faster and temps are dropping fast. The roads are getting dangerous. The Stone County Sheriff's Office is asking everybody to get where they're going and stay there until the storm passes. The kiddos will be thrilled because school is officially cancelled."

Heat pumped out of the vents, but it wasn't quite enough to cut the chill inside the Jeep now that the sun was down. If he'd known he'd be coming into this kind of weather, he'd have switched to the hard top. But hell, it was sixty degrees at home last week. The cold didn't really phase Harrison. Nothing much did. Still, he'd get a fire going when he made it to the cabin and put together some kind of stew for dinner. The kind that stuck to your ribs and warmed you from the inside out. With that happy thought in mind, he rounded the switchback and began the final climb. Just another mile or so.

His headlights swept over the guardrail. Or what used to be the guardrail. What remained was a mangled twist of metal. New or old? He slowed. The ground was already coated in snow, but he could tell it was churned up beneath. His body coiled with tension as he stopped and put on his flashers. For a few long seconds, he sat in the driver's seat, hands tight around the steering wheel as he stared at that gap in the rail.

Memory crept in of another snowy mountain road. Of gunfire and blood. He'd made the wrong call and three of his men had paid the price.

Harrison shook his head to clear it. This wasn't Afghanistan. Not an ambush. Somebody had gone over the side.

Hand on the Glock 19 at his hip, he climbed out of the Jeep and trudged carefully through the accumulating snow to the edge of the road. Some forty or fifty feet down the slope, an older model Chevy SUV was nose down, taillights on. No smoke plumed from the exhaust. Was the driver injured? He checked his phone. No bars to call 911. Looked like he was on rescue duty. At least if everything went to shit, nobody would be impacted but him this time.

Returning to the Jeep, he popped the liftgate, shifting supplies around until he could get to the coil of climbing rope. He'd need more than that to get somebody else back up. Surveying his options, he added a couple of locking carabiners and some para-cord to his pockets and shut the Jeep. Working fast, he anchored the center of the rope to a tree and tossed both ends over before running the length through his legs, around his hip, and over his shoulder for an emergency rappel. Positioning himself at the edge, he slowly let out slack and made his way down the slope. It wasn't as steep as what he was accustomed to climbing, but he was grateful for the rope. The ground was slick as hell, and the snow was getting deeper by the minute. The trip down took longer than he liked. As he neared the Blazer, he heard faint sounds of music. Singing? Ears straining against the strange muffling silence of the snow, Harrison listened.

Was that...Whitney Houston?

"I wanna feel the heat with somebody before I freeze to death, please God."

Not Whitney. The driver was apparently conscious and had some pipes. Was she delirious? Did she have a head injury?

This close to the vehicle, he could see that she'd been saved by the trees. Wedged between two stands, they were the only thing that had kept the SUV from hurtling into a boulder fifteen feet below. But while they'd slowed the momentum, they'd also blocked all four doors.

Harrison worked his way around the trees to the front of the vehicle. He could just make out a woman in the driver's seat—still singing. No blood that he could see, but who knew what was going on below the dash or behind the spiderwebbed windshield. He reached out and rapped on the hood and the singing turned into a scream.

CHAPTER 3

Oh, my holy Jesus, the bear is attacking the car!

Ivy clutched at her chest, certain she was having a heart attack and her body would be found frozen, in this car, sometime in the spring.

The bear spoke. Wait, not a bear. A gigantic, bearded dude stood in the beam of her headlights.

Somehow that wasn't any better. Was he a crazy mountain man? One of those preppers? Some lunatic in need of a wife, who would kidnap her and hold her hostage, never to be heard from again?

"Are you okay?" His voice was muffled by the snow and the vehicle.

He didn't *sound* crazy. Squinting at him through the falling snow, Ivy didn't think he looked crazy either. But what did crazy look like, anyway? It wasn't always frothing at the mouth. Look at her Aunt Lucile. She was crazy as a Betsy bug and mean with it, and nobody'd ever know it to look at her.

"Lady, can you hear me? Are you all right?"

Get ahold of yourself, woman. Whoever this guy was, he wanted to help. Which was a damn sight better than freezing to death on this mountain.

"I'm okay. I can't get out."

"Are your legs pinned?"

He was big enough he looked like he could rip the vehicle apart with his bare hands. "No, the doors are just blocked." She'd been too afraid to move much for fear that a shift in weight would send her Blazer hurtling the rest of the way down the mountain.

"Is it just you?"

Ivy hesitated. Was he making sure there was only her to incapacitate? *Oh, get a grip! It's a rational question in a rescue situation.* "Just me."

"Sit tight."

Like she was gonna do anything else?

He moved back into the trees. Where was he going? For help? Maybe they were close to a town and could call a tow truck. Would a tow truck even get out in all of this mess? *Could* a tow truck get her out?

She jolted again as he knocked on the back window.

"Unlock the doors."

Ivy's hand hovered over the auto lock. He could be a lunatic axe murderer.

A lunatic axe murderer, who just happened to drive by an hour after you went over and risked his life to climb down, on the off chance he'd find somebody to kill? You are paranoid, my dear. This is further proof you made the right decision in not writing romance.

She hit unlock.

Her rescuer wrestled with the back hatch for a minute before popping the liftgate window. "The back's jammed, but the window will open. You'll need to climb out this way."

Ivy was still in the driver's seat. "Is it safe to move? What if the car rocks and slides further?"

"It's wedged pretty good. I don't think it's going anywhere. Either way, it's not safe for you to stay here." The low rumble of his voice was matter-of-fact and strangely soothing. He was clearly a man used to giving orders. "Just move slow and steady."

Searching for some kind of calm, she unbuckled her seatbelt and immediately fell onto the steering wheel and the deflated airbag. "Oooph."

"You okay?"

"Probably bruised from the seatbelt. Could've been a lot worse."

With excruciating care, Ivy worked her way out of the driver's seat and over the center console so she could retrieve her purse from where it had landed in the floorboard. The SUV groaned a little but didn't move. Her phone had ended up on the far side of the dash, well out of range while she'd been pinned in the driver's seat. She groped for it now, stretching her fingers across the vinyl until they closed around the case.

Her crow of victory was cut short as she saw the screen matched the spiderwebbing of the windshield. It didn't light at the press of the home button. Great. She really was at the mercy of this stranger. Tossing the ruined phone into her purse, she shoved it through the gap between the front seats and hauled herself over the console, into the back.

Her bags had flown forward in the crash. Oh, dear God, her laptop! Not that there was anything worth a damn on the current book, but she had years of ideas accumulated on that hard drive. Resisting the urge to try to open the case and check, she looped the strap over her head and wore the bag cross-body. She looked at the suitcase, currently lying at the base of the driver's seat.

So lucky that didn't hit my head.

"If I shove my suitcase up, can you grab it?"

The grumpy lumberjack—it was what he looked like in the flannel shirt and shearling trucker jacket, with that thick, dark beard—made a grunt she took as assent. It took some doing to wrestle the bag ahead of her and push it up and over the backseat, so he could reach across the cargo space and grab it. But though the Blazer creaked and groaned, it didn't actually move. That made Ivy feel better.

Climbing out herself took a little more effort. She felt like a fish, flopping over the back of the seat in a graceless heap. The motion jarred the assortment of bruises starting to make themselves known in the wake of fading adrenaline. Her hands were shaking as she curled them over the edge of the liftgate and stood against the back of the second row seat. It was just enough to get her head and shoulders out of the SUV.

"Anything hurt? Broken?" the lumberjack asked.

"I don't think so."

"Good." Before she could do so much as blink, he slid his massive hands beneath her arms, plucked her right out of the Chevy, and set her down.

Ivy's feet immediately splayed like a baby deer. Instinctively, she curled her hands into his jacket and hung on. His arms tightened around her, effectively pulling her closer as he steadied them both. She was frozen through, but she'd have sworn she felt the heat of him through all their layers of clothes. He was just so *big* and *solid*. Her heart kicked into a fresh gallop, this time from something other than fear, as she held on longer than she should.

Too embarrassed to meet his eyes, she turned her gaze toward the Blazer. The blood drained out of her head, leaving her dizzy as she took in exactly how precarious her position had been. "Holy shit. That's bad."

"It's all right. You're safe. I've gotcha." Though his voice was brusque, his hold on her was surprisingly gentle.

Ivy risked looking up at his face. She couldn't see much in the almost dark, past that mountain man beard. His mouth was pulled into a frown and his dark brows drew together over dark eyes that seemed to look right through her. Her skin flushed.

"Thank you." Flustered, she planted her feet and pushed away, though he didn't actually let her go until she was stable. "Did you see the bear?"

He tensed. "What bear?"

"There was a bear in the road. I swerved to avoid it."

"Probably long gone now."

Ivy blew out a breath. "That's a relief. Maybe there will be enough signal up top to call a...wrecker." She trailed off as she realized exactly how far up the top really was. The glow of headlights illuminated the edge far, far above their heads. It wasn't straight vertical, but near enough. "How the hell did you even get down here?"

"Rappelled."

She scanned him, looking for a harness. "With no gear?"

"I've got climbing rope."

And obviously he knew what he was doing if he'd made it all the way down here, but still. "You could've broken your neck."

His lips curved just a little, as if he found the idea of that amusing. "I didn't."

Something about that cockiness had a hysterical laugh bubbling up in her throat. What if this was all a hallucination? What if she'd gotten a concussion during the wreck and her mind had conjured up Michael Keenan himself to rescue her? He looked about like she thought Michael would since he'd gone off the grid. What if, even now, she was still trapped in that front seat, bleeding to death from a head wound?

He was talking again. "—no way a wrecker could even get out right now. There wouldn't be enough traction in these conditions to actually pull your vehicle out. And that's assuming they can actually get it out at all. Snow's just getting worse and town is twenty miles away. We need to get out of here and to shelter. My cabin's not far."

A prickle of worry skittered across her skin. He wasn't wrong. She'd freeze to death if she stayed out here. If this wasn't a hallucination, that meant she'd be trapped with this guy in the middle of freaking nowhere for who knew how long. She didn't know this man, her phone was toast, and she had no other option but to trust him. He'd risked his life for an absolute stranger, not even knowing whether someone was in the car. Surely, that was another check in the Not An Axe Murderer column.

And, come on, this was Tennessee. The snow couldn't last that long.

Working up what she hoped was a confident smile, Ivy looked at the rope he'd evidently used to climb down. "Okay then. Lead the way."

~

THAT WAS a fake-it-til-you-make-it smile if Harrison had ever seen one. He'd been running ascent scenarios since he got her out of the SUV. She was shaky but not terribly injured, best he could tell. Her red wool coat and jeans were meant for the city, but at least she wasn't wearing some ridiculous high-heeled shoes or designer boots. The rubber-soled Wallabees would give some decent traction. The safest way would be to send her up first.

"You ever do any rock climbing?"

She went brows up. "Does the climbing wall at the gym back in college and grad school count?"

She couldn't be that far out of school. "Better than nothing." He pulled out the para-cord and began to uncoil it. "I'm gonna fashion an emergency harness for you and belay you up the incline."

"You're gonna trust my weight to *that?*"

"It holds my weight, so you'll be nothing. It won't be comfortable, but it'll do the job." Quick and efficient, he had the knots tied by the time he finished speaking and stepped toward her with the loop.

The woman took half a step back. "We're gonna climb up there *in the dark?*"

"Look, lady, I'm not gonna freeze my ass off out here. The way out is up." It wasn't full dark yet, but it would be soon, and he felt too damned exposed.

She hesitated but evidently decided he was a better alternative to hypothermia. She gave a slow nod. Her hands—scraped from the airbag deployment probably—were white-knuckled around the strap of her bag as he stepped toward her again.

Good job, Wilkes. Terrify the accident victim.

Sucking in a breath, he made an effort to pull himself back from the edge of memories he'd been skating. Not Afghanistan. Not a trap. She was just a woman in the wrong place at the wrong time, and she was scared. Her very real fear helped dissolve some of his. He could be a slightly less grumpy bastard.

"So, you saw a bear?" Maybe getting her to talk would help distract her from what he was doing.

"Yeah. I came around the curve and it was right there, in the middle of the road. I fishtailed when I swerved and spun right out through the guardrail. I don't know what the heck it was doing there. I thought they were supposed to hibernate in the winter." Her teeth chattered, likely with shock as much as cold. He needed to get her to shelter and out of the elements.

Harrison held up the loop again. "I've got to get up in your personal space to do this, okay?" When she nodded again, he reached around to loop the cord behind her waist. "I don't think that's necessarily the case with bears this far south. It was in the fifties just two weeks ago. Either way, you were damned lucky the trees were thick."

"Yeah."

Her accent was Southern, but not the twang of East Tennessee. He couldn't quite place it. "I'm guessing you aren't from around here." Reaching between her legs, he pulled the cord up to meet the loops he held in his other hand.

"There's not a lot of snow where I'm from."

Harrison forgot what he'd asked because he suddenly became very aware that the body in front of him was female. She was so tiny and delicate, and she smelled, impossibly, of honeysuckle. The scent of it cut through whatever dark memories lingered, grounding him with an unexpected flash of heat.

When was the last time he'd been this close to a woman?

Struggling to bring himself back to the task at hand he tried to remember what he'd said. "There's not normally this much snow here, either. Not like this."

"I certainly didn't expect a blizzard in Tennessee."

"The weather people were calling it Stormageddon."

"Great." The absolute lack of enthusiasm almost made him smile.

He locked down the carabiner and adjusted the fit of the makeshift harness. It was too dark to see her well, but he had the feeling she was blushing as he tugged and arranged the lines around her excellent ass. He should not be noticing her ass.

Clearing his throat, he straightened. "Okay, here's how this is going to work."

By the time he'd explained it and had her repeat the procedure back to him to his satisfaction, it really was full dark. He didn't like it, but there wasn't much of an alternative.

"Ready?"

"As I'll ever be." She was freezing and probably still scared to death, but she didn't balk again. "Belay on."

Harrison's estimation of her went up a few notches. He braced his feet. "On belay. Take your time and be careful of your footing. If you slip, I'll catch you." That much he was capable of.

She began to climb. It wasn't a terrible incline. In the daylight, on a normal day, most novices in reasonable shape could probably take it without a rope. But in the dark, in the snow, with an accident victim suffering from exposure, shock, and unknown injuries... The harness would hold. He had faith in that. But a slip and fall would bang her up even more than the wreck already had, and under the circumstances, he couldn't get her up to the top fast or easily by himself. With every inch higher, he adjusted his grip, cranking down on the lines, ready for the sudden jerk of her full weight.

But it didn't come.

She was careful, testing each foot placement before pushing up and giving it her weight. There were a handful of saplings growing along the steep grade, and she made excellent use of them as she hauled herself up the slope, muttering the whole way. The wind and snow muffled her words, but he heard something that sounded like "Suck it up, Buttercup. Annika would say this is a cake walk. She'd be doing it without ropes, just like Tom Cruise."

As she got higher, he lost the thread of her one-sided conversation. The last ten feet was the steepest part of the climb. If there'd been any small trees there to start, her SUV had wiped them out. She paused where she was, angling her head back, then pressing it against one forearm.

"Doing all right?"

"Fine. Just making deals with myself that I'll get to the gym more often in the future." She twisted to look down at him as she spoke and he saw the moment she recognized her mistake.

The line jolted as she hastily flattened herself against the rock face.

"You okay?"

After a moment's hesitation she called back, "It's a really long way down."

"Are you dizzy?"

"Little bit."

That could be vertigo or she might've hit her head in the crash. Either way, he needed to speed this process up. If she lost consciousness, they'd be up shit creek. Bad as the weather was getting, there'd be no going back to town tonight. Whatever first aid she required would be on him. The weight of that responsibility had his already tense muscles coiling tighter. He didn't want anybody relying on him for anything, least of all this woman.

"Just breathe for a minute." Harrison wasn't entirely sure which of them he was talking to.

He was running alternate scenarios in his head when she started climbing again, quicker this time, as if she needed to get to the top before she completely lost her nerve. Speed usually translated to carelessness. In his world, that meant people ended up hurt or dead. He didn't need another body on his conscience.

Don't slip. Don't slip. Don't slip.

He stayed silent, lest he distract her from what she was doing. When she bellied over the top edge of the road and disappeared from view, he almost cheered. The relief that she'd made it, that there were no further injuries, almost buckled his knees.

"Good job. Now unhook yourself from the line and toss your end of the rope down. We'll haul up your bags."

The rope trembled as she detached herself. "Hey, you have a winch on the front of your Jeep."

"I don't want to take the time to walk you through how to use it in this weather. Just toss the rope down."

One minute passed. Then two. No rope.

"Problem?"

No answer. Shit. Had she passed out?

He was just about to haul himself to the top, her luggage be damned, when he heard the faint whine of an electric motor. Damn woman didn't listen. She'd probably break something or burn out the motor...

Her head appeared over the side, dark hair whipping in the wind. "The winch will be faster."

The winch cable almost smacked him in the face when she tossed it over.

Well, I'll be damned.

Maybe she wasn't so much a damsel in distress as he'd first thought. She was capable and, despite her injuries, perfectly able to get her feet under her and turn around to help him. Somehow that was a relief, too. She might've been able to rescue herself once she'd gotten up the nerve. Which meant she didn't really need him at all. She'd just needed a helping hand.

It was a good reminder from the universe that it wasn't actually his job to save everyone anymore.

Thank God.

CHAPTER 4

By the time they reached his cabin almost an hour later, Ivy was so cold, she was beyond hurting with it. For the moment, that was a good thing. The numbness probably masked some pain from the wreck itself. What dexterity she'd had in her hands during the climb was gone as her fingers turned into blocks of uncooperative ice. It took her three tries to get the passenger door open, and by the time she did, her rescuer was already on the porch unlocking the place. She stepped out of the Jeep and nearly went down as a wave of dizziness swept over her.

Shock. She was in shock.

Not really a surprise but unfortunate. Given she had, improbably, been rescued by a man with a certain set of skills, she wished she could keep her wits about her. Not only because he was a stranger but because it seemed as if God had hand-delivered the perfect subject for observational research on her taciturn, uncooperative hero. This guy might look like a lumberjack, but she'd bet her next advance check he was former military and knew how to use that Glock she'd noticed on his hip. She hadn't decided whether she needed to worry about that or not. It was taking a lot of energy to stay awake.

Really, she should try to take notes about the subjective experience. It would make for great detail to add into her books...

Shaking off the haze, Ivy trudged up the steps.

Michael—she'd think of him as Michael until he gave her his actual name—entered the cabin like a man on a mission, moving fast. She half-expected him to yell, "Clear!" He went straight to the thermostat, presumably cranking it up.

The interior of the cabin was warmer than the outside but still plenty cold. It was nice to be out of the wind. She could see the whole of it from the front door. A main living area with vaulted ceilings bled into a corner kitchen. A steep, narrow staircase led up to what looked like a loft sleeping space. The area below that was walled off, probably for a bathroom.

"I'm gonna get a fire going. You think you can make coffee?"

"Sure." Glad to have a task to keep herself moving, Ivy made her way over to the kitchen as he headed back outside. Probably she should take off her coat. It was soaked through from snow and the thin wool was more fashionable than functional, but the effort of shrugging it off felt like too much. Coffee first. Flexing her numb fingers, she began opening cabinet doors, looking for coffee supplies. She found an unopened can of Maxwell House and reached for it.

Something in the cabinet chittered and *moved*.

Ivy screamed, stumbling back and landing hard on her ass.

Before she could draw breath to scream again, there was a big, badass, *armed* lumberjack between her and whatever was hiding in the cabinet. Where the hell had he come from? He looked fierce and deadly and a little bit terrifying with that wickedly sharp combat knife in his hand. And something in his gaze told her he wasn't entirely here. Whatever he was seeing wasn't the critter that had startled her.

His breath hissed in and out. Sweat beaded his temple. For long moments, he held poised on the balls of his feet, ready for action. Ivy didn't dare move or speak.

A box of something fell out of the cabinet and a furry paw wrapped around the edge of the shelf.

Michael blinked, shaking his head as if to clear it, then sheathed the knife. "Looks like we've got a raccoon." Stripping off his coat, he slowly approached the cabinet, fabric outstretched.

Ivy crab-walked back around the edge of the counter, not wanting to be anywhere near that thing if it got loose. Weren't raccoons carriers of rabies?

Her concern, as it turned out, was unwarranted. Michael captured their intruder without much fanfare, carting the wriggling bundle of his coat outside. With the threat neutralized, Ivy tried to get to her feet, but her legs wouldn't cooperate and her body had somehow tripled in weight. Really, the floor wasn't so bad. Maybe if she had a nap...

Someone swore.

Abruptly, Ivy found herself scooped up in a pair of strong arms. She wished she were more alert to appreciate it, but she was so tired. At least she wasn't shivering anymore. He deposited her on a sofa and, with surprising gentleness, eased off her coat.

She sighed. "Thanks, Michael."

His hands paused. "It's Harrison."

Harrison. Well that was fitting. Her personal hero shared a name with the actor who played her favorite movie hero. That should make for good dreams.

"I should've asked before. What's your name?"

"Ivy."

"Well, Ivy, we have to get you out of these wet clothes. You're still losing body heat."

"Haven't even bought me dinner first." Even she could hear the slur of her words. That was probably a bad sign.

She thought she saw that faint curve of his mouth again in that God-awful beard.

With the same efficiency he'd shown at everything else, Harrison stripped off her jeans, then her sweater, leaving her in nothing but her plain cotton underwear, one of her comfy bras, and a tank top. Dimly, she regretted it wasn't satin and lace. At least it wasn't the holey underwear or granny panties. There was nothing salacious in his touch, not even anything appreciative in his gaze. He was all business. When had that started to seem like a pity?

Dragging a blanket off the back of the sofa, he wrapped her in it like a burrito. "Sit tight. I'm going to get the fire going."

Because keeping her eyes open seemed like a lot of work, she let them drift shut. What seemed like a moment later, he was tugging at the blanket.

"Wha—?"

"The fire's caught, but it'll take a bit to really put out some heat. There aren't any heat packs here so you've got me."

He scooped her up again, turning to settle them both back on the sofa. Suddenly she was chest to very naked, very warm chest with Harrison. In a few deft moves, he'd cocooned them both in the blanket, adding another to the pile before settling with his powerful arms wrapped around her.

"Um." She didn't dare open her mouth to say more than that.

"I know it's a little awkward, but try to relax. You'll warm up soon."

Ivy was pretty sure if she'd gotten a gander at him stripping down for this duty, her temperature would've spontaneously shot up a good fifteen degrees just from watching. Because the body twined with hers was *built*. She could feel the ridges of sculpted muscle beneath her cheek and hands. She wished this were something more than medically-necessary snuggling because his was the kind of body she'd love to explore by touch and taste.

What is wrong with you? This man risked his life to save yours, and he's only here with you because you're more than half-frozen. He's not making a pass at you.

But oh, as she felt the warmth of him begin to seep into her chilled flesh, a part of her wished he would.

As she drifted off again, she mused, *Maybe I did get a head injury.*

～

Ivy's chest rose and fell against his, a slow, deliberate rhythm that assured Harrison the danger was past. The warmth of her breath against the hollow of his throat was an anchor against the barrage of feelings assaulting him. It had been longer than he cared to remember since he'd been this close to a mostly naked woman. But it wasn't the edge of arousal at the feel of all that skin pressed to his that was messing with his head. That was just a physical response to proximity, and he was a guy who hadn't had sex in a long time.

He'd been doing a job when he stripped her down. Taking the next steps to get her warm in he safest way possible. He hadn't been prepared for what it would feel like to hold her. Hadn't been ready for how that gradual relaxation as she slipped into sleep would fire up every protective instinct he had. Because sleep like this was a kind of trust. One he didn't have in himself and didn't feel like he deserved. She'd trusted him enough to have her back that she'd let go to do what her body needed to do.

That faith felt really damned good.

He hadn't let himself get close to anyone since he separated from the Army. He hadn't even been able to acknowledge to himself that he needed that. But the intimacy of this situation with Ivy forced him to recognize he was starved for human touch, for connection. He sure as hell shouldn't be looking for it with this woman, who would blow out of his life as suddenly as she came into it, as soon as weather permitted. But holding her, feeling her body slowly warm from his, knowing he'd give whatever protection she needed, left him with a bone-deep level of want that went so far beyond sex.

And that scared the hell out of him.

Ivy shifted against him, stretching with a little moan that was half-sexy, half-adorable before snuggling in closer, her lips brushing against his throat. That edge of arousal sharpened, giving him a far more immediate problem to deal with. He wracked his brain, cycling through baseball statistics and character lists from the books he'd been forced to read in high school English, in an effort to will his erection away. Ivy shifted again, one leg slipping between his, her knee sliding up perilously close to his balls, the ice block that was her foot dragging up the back of his calf. That worked where boredom inducement had not.

He knew the moment she really woke up. She went stock still, her body stiffening against his. Regret trickled through him as she slowly unwound her leg and eased back as far as his hold would allow—which wasn't far. He couldn't quite make his arms release her.

"Hi." Her voice was raspy from sleep and had his dick making another bid for some action.

Harrison didn't move, lest he draw attention to it. "Hi."

Ivy tipped her face back to look at him. The eyes that met his were a clear, silvery-green that made him think of tromping through snowy woods and cutting down Christmas trees. Her cheeks had a pretty pink flush he suspected it was from embarrassment rather than cold.

She cleared her throat, the color in her cheeks going deeper. "So, you're here."

"I am."

"I thought I had a head injury and hallucinated you."

He couldn't stop himself from reaching out to brush the silky dark hair back from her temple, ostensibly to get a better look at the small cut there but really because he just needed to see what her hair felt like against his fingers. "You've got a little bruise here, but I don't think it's that kind of head injury."

Ivy's breath caught and his gaze darted to her face.

"Does that hurt?"

"No." Her voice was a little breathless and her pupils sprang wide.

They snared him, drawing him in as effectively as a tractor beam.

Bad idea.

Needing to put them back on some kind of even keel, he withdrew his hand, returning it to her back. "How many of me are there?"

"Oh, I have a feeling there's definitely only one," she muttered.

He caught the laugh rumbling in his chest before it could spill out. "You're probably not concussed. How are you feeling?"

"Tired. Sore. Stiff. Kinda hurts to move."

"Don't rush on my account." Shit. Did that really just come out of his mouth? He should be getting up, getting her some painkillers, letting her get dressed, getting some food in her. But before he could say any of that, she slowly settled her head back into the crook of his shoulder.

An awkward silence descended.

Now what?

"Well," she sighed, "I sure didn't expect to end up here when I ran away this afternoon."

Harrison went rigid, his arms tightening around her, those protective instincts roaring. Was there a boyfriend or husband who'd used his fists on her? The idea of it had him running mental inventory on what weapons he had at his disposal. Not that he needed anything more than his hands.

"Did someone hurt you?" He knew his voice was one step above a growl, but he couldn't seem to stop it. There was no excuse, ever, for raising a hand to a woman.

Oddly, his anger seemed to make her relax again. "No. I'm running away from work."

Whatever he'd expected, it wasn't that, but it didn't make him want to stand down. "What kind of work makes you run away?"

She tipped her head back again, her lips curving into a self-deprecatory smile. "I'm a writer, and I've missed a deadline. Well, not quite yet, but I'm close to missing it."

A writer. What were the odds? "Running away helps with that?"

"Getting away from the source of the stress and having a change of scenery seemed like a magnificent idea when I got in the car. I figured I'd relax a little and that seeing somewhere new would shake something loose. I hoped it would buy me some time to finish the book, so when I got back to civilization, I'd have something to give to my agent and editor, who have been hounding me for several weeks now."

Which probably just made the writer's block worse. Escaping all that seemed like a reasonable strategy. "How much do you lack?"

"Oh, all of it." Her tone was entirely off-hand, as if not having started and already being past deadline was no big deal.

Harrison arched a brow.

Ivy just shrugged and set her cheek back against his shoulder. "I've got the world's worst case of writer's block."

Her silky hair spilled over his arm. The whisper of it over his skin made his fingers itch to touch it again. To thread through the strands so he could tip her head back and find out if she tasted as good as she smelled and what she'd feel like if they got even closer.

Stand down, soldier. Harrison wasn't entirely sure if the mental order was to his errant cock or the rest of him. Christ almighty, when was the last time he'd been this fixated on a woman? Because neither part of him seemed inclined to follow orders—he was still thinking about her naked—he began unwinding their blanket cocoon. The cabin had warmed considerably since their arrival, and she was no longer in danger. There was no reason to maintain their proximity. No matter how good it felt.

"You should get some fluids, some painkillers. If that stays down, we'll see how you do with some food. I've got the fixings for soup." Harrison swung his legs to the floor, careful to shield his lap from Ivy's view.

"I don't want to intrude."

He couldn't stop the snort of laughter at that. "I think we're past that kind of formality. And either way, we're stuck here at least until morning. The snow hasn't done anything but get heavier while you were out."

Rising, he slipped into his jeans, subtly tucking away the evidence of his inappropriate thoughts.

Ivy didn't speak again until he slid on his shirt. "I'm sorry."

Surprised, he looked over his shoulder at where she'd sat up on the sofa, her lower half blessedly covered by the nest of blankets. "Why?"

"Because nobody comes to a place like this if they want company. So I'm sorry to have intruded on your solitude."

Shoving his feet back into his boots, he considered his reply. "You're not wrong. But sometimes whatever you're trying to escape by coming to a place like this is better held at bay by distraction. And you're definitely that." Lifting his head, he caught the flash of raw empathy in her eyes. Uncomfortable, he pushed to his feet. "Besides, it's not like you went over the edge on purpose."

"No, but you did. You saved my life. Thanks for that. For all of this."

Not wanting any credit, he shrugged. "You'd have gotten up the guts to get out before long."

"I'm not sure I'd have scaled the side of the mountain without you. So the thanks holds."

Grunting an acknowledgement, he crossed to the door. "I'll bring in all our bags."

Not daring another glance in her direction, he stepped into the swirling snow and hoped it would be more effective than a cold shower.

CHAPTER 5

*I*vy couldn't shake the feeling that Harrison was escaping her. Was it her thanks or that moment of connection? Maybe both. She'd hit on something, and he'd said more than he meant to. But she recognized him. Recognized the kind of man he was. She'd written men like him. Studied them. And knew that they didn't get that look in their eyes without ghosts riding their shoulders.

"Sometimes whatever you're trying to escape by coming to a place like this is better held at bay by distraction. And you're definitely that."

She didn't know what to think about that. Did he mean the rescue and just having her in his space? Or did he mean something else? Did she want him to mean something else? Her still puckered nipples certainly came down on the side of *oh hell yes.*

The front door opened and Harrison hustled back through, laden with bags. A gust of cold air and a swirl of snow blew in behind him and had Ivy hunching back into the blankets still warm from his body. She already missed the feel of him wrapped around her and regretted the loss of that temporary intimacy. It had felt so good to be held, to be touched. Not from a sex standpoint—though certainly it was hard not to think about that when he was so…swoon-worthy—but just as closeness to someone else. Which just went to show how isolated she'd gotten in the last year. She needed to get a handle on this because it was wholly inappropriate for her to be macking on her host when the attraction clearly wasn't reciprocated.

Suddenly acutely aware she was still without pants, Ivy wished for a little escape herself. She needed some space to get her head back on straight. "Would you mind if I took a shower?"

"No. Go ahead. I'll bring in the rest of the stuff and get dinner going." He set her bag just inside the bathroom doorway.

"Thanks." Feeling a little foolish, she wrapped a blanket around her waist. He'd already seen everything. But he hadn't been actively looking, and he'd been distracted by her prospective hypothermia.

As soon as he headed back outside for the rest of the stuff, she made a shuffling dash for the bathroom, dragging the blanket with her. It was rustic but clean, with shiplapped walls and a tub-shower combo on the other side of the toilet. There were navy towels beneath the sink to match the plain navy shower curtain. She was surprised not to see camouflage everywhere, but this apparently wasn't like the hunting cabins she'd been to growing up. There was craftsmanship here. His? Or someone else's?

Shrugging off the question, she dropped the blanket and turned on the water to warm before stripping out of the rest of her clothes. She froze as she caught her reflection in the mirror. Angry bruising ran from her left shoulder, across her body, all the way down to her right hip. That was gonna be ugly for a while. But it could have been so much worse. Now that the adrenaline had faded, she was beginning to feel every ache and pain. No doubt that would become more pronounced over the next few hours. Painkillers were definitely in order. But shower first.

She stepped beneath the spray. Her skin woke up with a scream as sensation returned. Ivy stayed where she was and let the water sluice over her body. Once the initial pain was past, she closed her eyes and leaned against the front wall, glorying in the luxury of warmth. With warmth came clarity.

She was trapped for the foreseeable future, in a cabin with no means of contacting the outside world, with a guy who was still a veritable stranger. It sounded like the setup for one of the victims in her books or maybe a horror novel. And yet she wasn't afraid of Harrison. Maybe that was somewhat her neglected hormones talking because she'd been next to naked with him, but she didn't think so. Even with that moment in the kitchen, where he was clearly not entirely present, maybe seeing some of those ghosts he was running from, she hadn't been afraid of him.

Yeah, he'd started out gruff and taciturn, but he'd been focused on getting them to safety, then on taking care of her—something he hadn't asked for but hadn't begrudged or complained about. He'd been respectful and gentle, doing everything that needed to be done, including using his own body to warm her. That had been...frankly...amazing and had left her wanting a helluva lot more than a snuggle. And, at least for a bit there, so had he.

But he was a guy and they'd been almost naked together. His arousal was probably more about proximity and biology than actual attraction. Yet he'd softened toward her. He'd had such gentleness in his touch when he'd brushed the hair back from her face. She'd wanted to close that little distance between them. Wanted to kiss him and feel the scrape of his beard along her skin. And then there was that protective streak. He'd been all kinds of ready to take on someone who'd hurt her. It spoke volumes about the kind of man he was. The kind she found appealing on multiple levels.

Feeling almost human again, Ivy stepped out of the shower and toweled off.

That contrast of gentle caretaker and fierce protector intrigued her. She'd written plenty of fierce men, and her share of women, too. But she'd never really explored a softer side to any of them. There was little room for softness in their line of work.

Death and darkness didn't exactly inspire it. And yet she had the sense that Harrison had seen his share of death and darkness, and he still had that capacity for gentleness. It made her think of Michael and wonder what—or who—it would take to soften him.

Was that what was missing? A situation to show another side of him? A window into something besides the wound that had made him leave the team?

Mulling it over, she stepped out of the bathroom to the scent of food. Following her nose into the little kitchen, she peeked into the pot simmering on the stove. It seemed like some kind of soup —the kind where you browned a pound of ground beef and dumped in a can of every vegetable you had. The scent of it had her stomach growling. It had been far too long since those snack cakes on the road. On the counter, she found a glass of water and a bottle of painkillers, but Harrison himself wasn't inside.

The thunk of an axe hitting wood drew her attention to the window. In the glow of a floodlight, Harrison tossed the split pieces onto a pile and placed another log on a tree stump. He wound up the swing and brought the axe down with an economy of motion that suggested he had plenty of practice. She watched him repeat the movement several more times, admiring the power of those broad shoulders and thick arms. She never would've imagined she had a thing for lumberjacks, but even with the over-grown beard, this whole mountain man picture was working for her.

A whole lot about Harrison was working for her.

And when did you start writing romance in your head?

Apparently about the time a big, burly stranger woke up my neglected libido.

Rolling her eyes at her own imaginings, Ivy retrieved her laptop case and braced herself for the worst. But the screen was intact. And when she pushed the power button, it sprang to life with no problems. It had survived the wreck. Thank God.

Wanting to capture some of her thoughts about Michael, she

opened a fresh document and began to type. She was still working when Harrison opened the door sometime later, a bundle of logs under one arm. Ivy couldn't help watching as he crossed the room to dump the wood into the wire basket by the fireplace, then wandered into the kitchen to check the soup. She managed to jerk her attention back to the screen, away from his denim clad ass just before he turned.

"Doing okay?"

"Yeah. Getting hungry. The water's stayed down." Because thinking about that ass had made her mouth go dry, she picked up the water she'd refilled and drank more of it.

He nodded. "We should have plenty of firewood to get us through the night. I'll go shower off and then we'll eat."

"Sounds good."

He disappeared into the bathroom. Ivy tried to get back to work, but whatever groove she'd managed to find seemed to have deserted her. Her head felt scrambled. She wished she could blame it on the accident or on Harrison himself, but she knew it had been going on so much longer. She'd been mentally blank, going through the motions for so long, she was starting to worry that this wasn't writer's block.

Abandoning the laptop, she curled up in the chair by the fireplace, staring into the flames and brooding. What if whatever the hell was going on with her head couldn't be fixed? What if she was permanently broken? What if her career was over? The idea of it left a sick feeling in her gut. She loved her job. Or she had before it started to feel like opening her manuscript was tantamount to making a gallows walk.

The bathroom door opened. Ivy lifted her head in reflex, then blinked in confusion at the stranger who emerged, clad in a darker pair of jeans and yet another flannel shirt.

Holy shit.

He'd shaved the beard. Not all the way off, but he'd definitely attacked it with trimmers, knocking off several inches of ZZ Top wannabe and leaving him with a close-cropped beard that high-lighted his strong jaw. It made him more approachable and...well, incredibly hot. Turned out the face that he'd been hiding under-neath all that hair was as gorgeous as the well-toned body.

Perilously close to drooling, Ivy realized he'd said something to her. "I'm sorry, what?"

"I asked if you were getting any work done."

She couldn't stop the snort of disgust. "No. Not really."

He dumped his dirty clothes into a bag and padded into the kitchen. "You wanna talk about it?"

Her first instinct was a resounding no. Because what good would talking about it do? But watching him at the stove, she reconsidered. What little inspiration she'd cobbled together had been because of him. She wanted to know more about him. Sharing something of herself might get him to let down his walls again. And maybe, just maybe, she'd find the piece she'd been missing for her plot.

~

"I USED TO LOVE MY JOB."

There was so much longing in her tone, Harrison had to fight the urge to hug her. And what the hell was up with that? But he understood what it felt like—to have that high of being blessed enough to do the thing you felt like you'd been born to do, and the corresponding low when it all fell apart. He'd loved being a Ranger. Until he hadn't.

"You said you're a writer." Better to get his brain back on her and her issues.

"That's what it says on my résumé. I'm not feeling much like one lately." She accepted the bowl of soup he passed her and went to sit at the little dinette table.

He followed with his own bowl and a sleeve of crackers. "Written anything I'd have heard of?" Probably not. She looked young. Not jailbait young, but definitely not over thirty, like he was. He pegged her for a romance writer or maybe young adult.

"Maybe." She restlessly stirred her soup, as if that would make it cool faster, and didn't meet his eyes.

Harrison waited for her to elaborate, but she said nothing. He wasn't used to having someone wait him out, and her reticence had his curiosity piqued. "Are you embarrassed or worried this is gonna turn into a *Misery* kind of situation?" As soon as the words were out, he winced. "Sorry, bringing up a writer who gets kidnapped and tied to a bed is probably in poor taste under the circumstances."

But it got her to look at him again. For just a moment, those silver-green eyes held an unmistakable glint of lust and intrigue that had Harrison's brain scrambling down an entirely different path than the one he'd been joking about. Shit, he hadn't had any intention of going there and now they were both thinking about the sofa and skin and...

Ivy pointed her spoon at him, her expression shifting to amusement. "You are no Annie Wilkes."

What would she say if he told her they shared a last name? Before he could ask, she continued.

"And I'm not embarrassed." The pretty flush of her cheeks belied her words, but that was probably about the inadvertent naked thoughts. Or maybe that was just wishful thinking on his part.

"What?" he teased. "Is it some of that Fifty Shades kind of sh— stuff?" What the hell was wrong with him, pursuing this line of questioning? When had he decided it was a good idea to flirt with this woman?

She made a disgusted face and shook her head with vehemence as she dug into the soup. "It is definitely not erotica. It's not even romance, although there are some romantic elements that have cropped up in the series. It's just that nice girls aren't supposed to write about gruesome things like serial murder."

Harrison didn't bother to mask his surprise. "You don't look like someone who'd write about something that dark."

One dark brow arched up. "And what does someone who writes about the ultimate darkness of the human heart look like? There are some who would say I'm extremely well-adjusted because I exorcise my less-acceptable impulses through fiction."

"So you're saying you have recurrent thoughts of homicide?"

She pointed her spoon at him. "Don't piss off the writer. She may put you in a book and kill you. As it happens, I've gotten fictional revenge on a looooot of people."

Beyond mildly curious now, he ripped open the crackers and pulled out a few. "What series?"

"The Sloan Maddox series."

The crackers fell out of numb fingers and into his soup as Harrison stared. "You're Blake Iverson?"

She gave a little shrug and a half smile. "Guilty."

Hollow Point Ridge, the final book in the series, was on his e-reader right now. "But everybody assumes you're a dude." Certainly the dark, gritty thrillers that were driving Jack Reacher fans wild did not in any way give hints of this tiny, gentle-looking woman.

"It's ridiculous, but there's wider marketability that way. Men are more likely to pick up a book by a guy than they are something by Ivy Blake. And since I refuse public appearances, nobody is any the wiser."

"Well, I'll be damned. So this book you're late on is the next Sloan Maddox? I thought book six was the end of the series."

Again with the head shake. "My publisher wants me to branch out. It's supposed to be the start of a new series featuring another character from the core series, but it's just not gelling."

"Which character?"

Her brow winged up. "You've read one of them?"

"I've read all of them. Well, I haven't finished the latest one yet. I had to set it aside just after they found the second body." Because he'd had to go bury another one. But he didn't want to bring that up right now. "I had intended to finish it tonight when I got here."

There went the blush again. Damn, she was cute. How did a woman like this turn out books that made his skin crawl?

"You have a dark and twisted mind." Too late, it occurred to him that she might be offended by that observation.

But Ivy just grinned. "Thanks. I might as well get some use out my graduate degree."

"Which is in what?"

"Forensic psychology."

Harrison blinked, surprised yet again. "Seriously?"

She inclined her head and shrugged, as if to say "Guilty."

"What were you originally gonna do with that?"

"I had a notion of eventually going into the FBI and the Behavioral Analysis Unit. I'm fascinated by the criminal mind. But I'm way less okay with going out in the field, which I discovered during a very brief relationship with a homicide detective while I was in grad school. He got called to a scene while we were out, and I was a dumbass who didn't follow orders and stay in the car. I knew when I saw my first—and only—homicide victim, I'd never hack it as an actual member of law enforcement. It takes a special kind of tough to do those jobs, and I don't have it."

"You'd never know it from your books. Some of your serial killers have given me nightmares." And he'd been relieved when her characters' darkness had choked out his own.

Ivy beamed. "Thanks."

"I, for one, am glad you took a different path." He hated the idea of her losing her softness. Though given the sort of books she wrote, maybe that was an illusion. How could someone understand darkness that well and still remain any kind of innocent?

"You and my parents both. They always hated the idea of me being FBI."

"Dangerous job. It's a parent's prerogative to hope their kid doesn't do something that's liable to get them shot." His mom certainly hadn't been keen on him going into the Army. She'd been proud of his service but terrified the whole time. She'd thrown a huge party when he decided not to re-up.

"Why did you want to do it?" He couldn't imagine this petite woman in the soft sweater and well-worn jeans with the formal bearing and bland suit of a federal agent.

"I'm good at reading people. I guess that came from moving around a lot, always being the new kid in class."

"Were you a military brat?"

"Preacher's kid. The Methodist Church likes to move its ministers every few years within the jurisdiction. So I've lived all over the southeastern US. When you're always the new kid, it's handy to be able to size people up in a hurry. Figure out where you might best fit in."

"True enough, but it's a long way from new kid in school to FBI." There had to be some bigger reason than simply curiosity.

Ivy flashed a self-deprecatory smile. "You're wondering if I have some kind of trauma or something that prompted me to want to go out and get all the bad guys."

He should not play poker with this woman. "It seems the logical conclusion."

"Profiling isn't always about logic. Whether you're talking serial killers or regular people. I like the puzzle of trying to figure out what makes someone tick, and it turned out I had an aptitude for it."

Harrison thought of her earlier observation. *Nobody comes to a place like this if they want company.* No matter what she'd said about logic, that one wasn't difficult to puzzle out. But he wondered what else she'd uncover during their time together and wasn't at all sure he'd be comfortable with her insights.

Shrugging off his unease, he turned his attention back to their conversation. "So why not regular psychology? Why the criminal stuff?"

"For one thing, I have zero tolerance for everyday problems. A lot of therapy involves just listening to people bitch and never actually wanting to change. I'd have been miserable inside a year. But the bigger reason? Well, you'll think it's stupid."

"Try me."

"I saw reruns of this show from the late nineties. *Profiler.* The heroine was this forensic psychologist who worked for some fictional government division that partnered with assorted other agencies to bring down the perpetrators of violent crimes. I loved the crap out of that show. It fascinated me, and I thought what a great job. Taking down the bad guys by basically outsmarting them. After that I was hooked."

"You decided to join the FBI because of a TV show?"

"I told you you'd think it was stupid." The hunch in her shoulders suggested she'd gotten that reaction before.

"Not stupid. Just surprising."

"I don't have some noble reason for doing it. And, as it happened, I didn't have the stomach to do more than write about it."

"You're damned good at the writing of it, so there's hardly any shame in that. Not everything has to be done for some noble cause."

"Did you have some noble reason for going into the military?"

Harrison shouldn't have been surprised. She'd been sitting here talking about having studied to be a profiler. But the question sat him back in his chair. "That obvious?"

"That you were in the military? Yes. You rappelled down the side of a mountain in a Tennessee blizzard, by yourself, to help a perfect stranger and didn't even break a sweat."

Well, she'd been wrong about that part. Nice to know it hadn't shown. "It was a baby mountain and not anywhere approaching a real blizzard."

"Still. That's not a thing the average civilian is capable of or inclined to do. Plus, there's the way you move—with this total economy of motion, nothing wasted. And even if you hadn't broken out your badass search and rescue skills, there was your response to the raccoon. You thought I was in danger and you reacted with the kind of speed that only someone with considerable training can manage. So I'm betting you weren't just military, you were special forces."

Harrison's mouth went dry. If that was her takeaway from the raccoon incident, then maybe she wasn't quite as observant as she seemed. Or maybe he hadn't been as obvious as he'd thought. "How do you know I'm not still active?"

"Unless you were coming off of some posting where relaxed grooming standards were the norm, you had way too much beard for active military and your hair isn't military cut. I'd guess you've been out two or three years."

He wished he'd cracked open one of the beers in the fridge, but he wasn't about to betray himself by doing it now. He'd been trained to withstand torture. He could tolerate some discomfort from one incredibly intuitive woman.

CHAPTER 6

$\mathcal{H}$arrison's expression didn't change from that blank, neutral mask as he relaxed back in his chair, but Ivy didn't miss the faint tightening of his hand, as if he wished he were holding something.

"Well, I bet you're fun at parties."

His tone was dry but she knew she'd gone too far, treading at the edge of territory he clearly didn't want to discuss. So she swallowed down her speculation about why he might have left the military and reminded herself that this wasn't a character whose head she could crawl around in endlessly in the name of the story. This was a real-life man, who had the right to privacy. He'd confirmed enough of her suspicions.

Wanting to put him at ease again, she flashed a rueful smile and shifted the conversation back to herself. "I can't remember the last time I went to one. I'm something of a workaholic."

The subtle tightening around his mouth eased. "You said you used to love your work. You don't anymore?"

Ivy hesitated before answering. She didn't talk about this. Not with anyone. Certainly not a fan. Fan questions, in general, usually made her uncomfortable. But she had a feeling that Harrison's wouldn't be the simple, surface stuff that people so often asked. And probably she owed him this after trying to get into his head.

"I wrote my first book in grad school. It was something I did to blow off steam in between writing my master's thesis. I did it for fun because almost every time we discussed a profile in class, my brain spit out so much more than just the facts of an unknown subject. Building a story around it was instinctive and drove some of my professors crazy. But my classmates enjoyed it. I had kind of a little mailing list, I guess. I'd send out new chapters as I wrote them. It was a way for us all to be entertained in the middle of all the stress that goes along with grad school. And after I had my epiphany that I would not, in fact, be joining the ranks of the FBI, a friend suggested I polish up the book and try to get it published."

She spooned up some soup, more to have something to do with her hands than because she was still hungry. "I didn't hold out much hope that I'd get far with it, but I ended up landing an agent out of the first batch of query letters I sent. And six weeks after I signed, I found myself in the middle of a bidding war between three different publishers."

He shifted forward and began to eat again. "That must've been a helluva charge."

"It was. It was exciting. Everything my professors busted my chops over, editors loved. I accepted a three-book deal. They rushed the first book to market because it was more or less done, other than some minor revisions, and Wally—that's my editor— ordered me to get started on the second. I had it and the third book finished by the time the first one hit the *New York Times* best seller list. Those books poured out of me, like they'd just been waiting for an outlet. I've never had so much fun in my life. I was getting to tell the kind of stories I'd been making up for years and getting paid for it." Her lips curved at the memory.

"So what changed?"

The remembered excitement faded. "Books two and three

premiered on the *Times* list. My publisher asked for another three books in the series. And because I'd ripped out two and three at such a fast pace, they gave me pretty short deadlines, wanting to maximize on the momentum we'd started. It was a brutal, ruthless pace. But I was with it. I delivered. And I did all the things they asked of me. The social media and fan stuff. The blog tours. If my publicist told me to do something, I said yes ma'am. Literally the only line I drew was public appearances. I'm petrified of public speaking, and since they'd published me as Blake Iverson, they were cool with that. Maintaining the mystery, as it were.

"But book six was hard. Finding the balancing act between doing the research, getting the book written, keeping fans happy, doing all the social media crap so I wasn't forgotten in between releases...all that took a toll. The subject matter of *Hollow Point Ridge* was pretty dark, even for me, and took a lot out of me. I figured I'd be fine after a little break. And I was. For little while. Then my publisher came back with launch numbers and wanted a spinoff series focused on Michael. Being wise enough not to bite the hand that feeds me, I said yes. But this book is..." She trailed off, not knowing what to say about it.

"Is what?" Harrison prompted.

"It's...not."

His brows drew down. "Not hard?"

"No, it's not a book. I haven't been able to write it." Just thinking about it had additional tension knotting in her neck. Closing her eyes, she reached up to rub at it with both hands. "I've tried. I've come at it from every direction I can think of. But it's just not working. Nothing's working. And Marianne and Wally are breathing down my neck because I've already blown one deadline, and I keep putting them off because I can't admit the truth."

"You're burnt out."

The breath she'd held gusted out. "Oh my God, so much."

There was such relief in hearing someone else voice the thing that had been circling around her brain for weeks now.

Harrison leaned forward, resting his forearms on the table—and damn, she hadn't known she had a thing for forearms, but his were powerful, with a light dusting of dark hair down the back. And those hands—

"So, if I'm getting this right, you've been working your ass off non-stop for...well the last three years for your publishing career, some number of years before that in grad school, and generally burning the candle at both ends. Have you taken any downtime to legitimately recover from all that?"

Ivy could only laugh, and she knew it had an hysterical edge. But she couldn't help it. The idea of downtime was as ludicrous as pink elephants in tutus. "There's been no time."

"You know what happens in the military if you don't take adequate time to deal with your shit?"

She stopped laughing and found herself leaning toward him, cheek propped against her fist. "I'm guessing you're going to tell me."

"You flame out. Lose your edge." *People die.* He didn't say it, but the implication hung between them.

Was that what had happened to him? Ivy knew better than to ask.

"I haven't been given a whole lot of choice. Publishing is all about deadlines and very few of them take the author into account."

"If you don't speak up, they sure as hell never will."

He didn't understand. And yet... "You're not wrong. I need a break. A real, legitimate break. With no pressure about the book, no threat of my career imploding hanging over my head. But I have no idea how the hell I'm going to get it."

The corners of that surprisingly sensual mouth tipped up, just a little. "Well, you're currently trapped in a cabin with no wi-fi, no phone, and no way for anybody to reach you to bug you about it."

When exactly had that stopped feeling alarming?

"I am," she agreed.

"Maybe let yourself off the hook and take advantage of it."

As she sat across from this interesting, sexy guy, all she could really think about was taking advantage of him.

HE'D BEEN on the verge of suggesting she stay here for a little while. Much as he thought he'd wanted—needed—solitude, he was enjoying her company. He was so aware of her, there was no room to focus on anything else—like the very stuff he was trying to escape. But the words caught in his throat at the flash of hunger in her eyes.

His gaze dropped to her mouth, wondering how she'd taste and what those lips would feel like cruising over his skin. His body woke to attention, his hands itching to reach across the table and drag her into his lap. Her quickened breath and parted lips suggested she might be on board with that plan. When he managed to drag his focus back to her eyes, her pupils were blown wide.

This was a terrible idea. He tried to hang on to that fact as the tension and heat seemed to build in the space between them. Doing anything about this attraction, when there was no escape if it all went sideways, was a prime recipe for a shit show. And, fuck's sake, she'd been in an accident today.

But none of that stopped the wanting or dimmed the desire to lose himself and his lingering grief in the body he'd fought so hard not to notice. He wanted to touch and taste and take. To strip away her stresses and her secrets until she'd forgotten everything but him.

The lights went out.

Harrison jerked back from where he'd been leaning toward her, the sudden darkness snapping him out of the haze of lust before he did something he couldn't take back. If he felt some regret at that, well, it had been a long damned time since he'd wanted anyone this badly.

He could just see Ivy's silhouette in the glow cast by the fire.

"I'm guessing that's bad." Her tone was so bland and natural, he wondered if he'd imagined the heat in her gaze.

Struggling to get himself under control again, he shifted his attention to this newest wrinkle in his plans. "I'm actually surprised it took this long, given the volume of snow out there. The infrastructure around here isn't really prepared for this." Shoving back from the table, he made his way over to where he'd left his boots. "I'll go see about turning on the generator."

Ivy got up, too, reaching for the coat he'd hung up by the fire to dry out.

"What are you doing?" he demanded.

"Going with you."

"There is no reason for you to get frozen again." Although, if she did, they could share body heat again, preferably naked and active this time... *Get a grip, Wilkes.*

She frowned at him. "You might need somebody to hold a flashlight while you do...whatever you do to a generator."

"If I need that, I'll come back and get you." With the image of getting naked with her in more than medically-recommended ways still fogging his mind, he needed a few minutes to get his arousal under control. Or maybe more than a few. The cold ought to do that.

"Fine. I'll clean up the dinner dishes."

Grabbing a flashlight from his pack, Harrison headed outside. Porter had told him the generator was in a little lean-to off the back of the cabin. Trudging through the accumulated snow—there had to be a good five or six inches here already—he rounded the corner. Temperatures had to be hovering in the low twenties, with wind chills in the teens. It was gonna get damned chilly in a hurry if he didn't get this thing up and running.

Using the keys Porter had given him, he unlocked the lean-to and wrestled the door open. The generator was ready and waiting as advertised. He checked the fuel level and cables. Balancing the flashlight on the shelving unit holding assorted tools and equipment, he got a good grip on the handle of the crank cord and yanked. Nothing. Expecting that, he gave it a few more pulls. The motor sputtered and coughed, but refused to catch. Grabbing the flashlight, he made a closer inspection, trying to figure out the problem. The cables were intact. No signs of fraying or chewing by animals. Nothing else jumped out at him as the obvious culprit.

Shit.

Without more light, there was no way he could diagnose this thing. He could take Ivy up on her offer of assistance, but if he wasn't able to fix the generator and the power didn't come back on, she'd be getting cold for no reason, and no matter what his lower half thought about the idea, she didn't need to go through that again. Better to conserve the heat they had in the cabin now, and he'd sort everything out in the daylight tomorrow.

Gathering another huge stack of firewood, he tromped back inside. "So I've got good news and bad news. The bad news: Something's wrong with the generator. It won't crank. I can probably fix it, but it'll take a while, and I don't like my odds of missing something in the dark, so that should wait until tomorrow." He made a neat stack of the logs beside the wood basket and turned to face her. "The good news is that the water heater and range are gas, and we've got more than enough firewood to last us through the night."

"That doesn't sound so bad." Ivy's gaze slid upstairs. "And since heat rises, the loft should stay pretty warm as long as the fire's still burning, right?"

The loft. Which held the only bed in the place. And now he was back to willing away his hard-on. Damn it.

"Yeah, it ought to be okay up there. You can have the bed. I'll sleep on the sofa." He'd break his back and probably wouldn't sleep a wink, but at least by the fire he wouldn't freeze, and she'd be safe from his questionable control.

Hands on hips, she shot him an exasperated look. "Harrison, that's just stupid. You barely fit on the sofa. We're both adults, and I think we've already proved we're more than capable of sharing personal space and doubling up on blankets to conserve heat."

Was that what they'd proved on the sofa earlier? He was pretty sure he'd only proved he wanted to get her naked. Sleeping in the same bed with her, inches from that tempting skin, without being able to touch her, sounded like a recipe for a sleepless night of torture. But he couldn't see a reasonable way to refuse without admitting to the attraction it was probably best they ignore.

At least a sleepless night in a bed meant less pain to his back.

"All right. If you're sure you're comfortable with that."

"Why wouldn't I be?"

Why, indeed?

CHAPTER 7

*I*vy woke confused, warm and toasty on one side, freezing on the other. Dragging herself fully to consciousness, she realized she was plastered against Harrison, whose long, muscular body was like a furnace. She'd have been perfectly content with that state of affairs, except he'd dragged all the covers to his side of the bed and her ass was hanging out, her yoga pants no match for the frigid air.

If the fire was still going, it had died down to a smolder that wasn't doing anything to warm them up here. Pale light streamed through the windows. It was probably close to dawn, but in her book, that meant it was too damned early to be awake. Especially when there'd be no coffee on autobrew if she went down to the kitchen.

Part of her wanted to go back to sleep for a couple of hours and get back to the fabulous dream she'd been having. The one where Harrison had decreed they'd make their own heat for the night. Since she'd apparently totally misread signals from the actual man last night, the only action she was gonna get was with the dream version, so she had a vested interest in hitting dreamland again to see he delivered. But a bigger part wanted to lie here and luxuriate in being close to him. It wasn't the skin-on-skin she craved, but she could have this and let it be enough. She just wanted to be warm enough to enjoy it.

Carefully disentangling herself, Ivy leaned over Harrison and tried to inch the comforter back to her side of the bed. It was wedged beneath his chin. Holding her breath, she reached across him, curling her fingers in the blanket.

Abruptly, the bed heaved as Harrison jacked up. Faster than she could squeak, he flipped her onto her back, his big body pinning hers, his massive hands gripping her wrists almost to the edge of bruising as he pressed her arms into the mattress. His breath sawed in and out, and she knew in an instant that he wasn't seeing her. His expression was too feral, too angry.

Her heart thundered against her ribs. She needed to snap him out of it before he acted out against whatever enemy he was seeing.

"Harrison." Her voice came out breathy, barely above a whisper because he'd knocked the wind out of her.

He didn't even blink at his name.

Ivy tried to suck in a breath, but his weight on her chest made it hard to draw in more than the shallowest of inhales. "Harrison, wake up."

Nothing.

She had no leverage, no means of combating his bigger bulk to free herself. Left with no other choice, she did the only thing she could think of.

She kissed him.

The second her lips met his, he froze. Pressing the moment's advantage, she poured herself into the kiss, willing him to snap out of it, to recognize her. A shudder rippled through him and he angled his mouth against hers and kissed her back.

Oh.

She'd expected retreat, not fevered response, but she was help-less to resist as he traced the seam of her lips with his tongue. It was her turn to shudder as she opened her mouth to him, tangling her tongue with his. The taste of him flooded her, dialing every last one of her brain cells to want. She needed to be closer, but he still had her pinned. Then the hands restraining her wrists released and the pressure on her chest disappeared. She whimpered at the loss, then he he shifted, settling between her legs, the the weight of him pressing his erection against her core, and the whimper turned into a moan.

"Oh God, yes."

She thrilled at the feel of him, wrapping one leg around his hips to pull him closer, swiveling her hips in response.

"Ivy." Hearing her name growled in that desperate, possessive tone had her lifting to him, grinding against him to assuage the ache between her thighs. But it wasn't enough. They were both wearing too many clothes. Apparently, deciding the same thing, Harrison released her hands, dragging his down to her waist to tunnel beneath the several layers she'd worn to bed. His callused fingers scraped up her torso, a delicious friction that woke her nerve endings and left her desperate for more. More skin, more heat. Just...more.

Touch me. Please, dear God, touch me before I burn to ash.

He inched his way higher, taking her mouth again in a searing kiss that should have incinerated all the clothes between them. Ivy clutched him tighter, trying to wrap around him. Then his hand found her breast.

Yes!

Threading her fingers into his hair, she arched into the touch, loving how the breadth of his palm covered her. But she wanted more. Wanted skin against skin. Her hands scrabbled at his t-shirt, trying to tug it up. Breaking the kiss, he yanked it over his head, tossing it to the side, before performing some kind of Houdini magic on the multiple layers she still wore, stripping them off in one smooth yank until she lay with her chest bare.

Harrison froze, the heat in his expression fading.

No. No. Don't stop.

Ivy reached for him, but he was already pulling back, yanking his hands from her body so fast, she almost felt a breeze. He rolled away, sitting up, his back to her. Adrift, confused, she couldn't quite move, still so turned on and unsatisfied, she could barely process what was happening. His ragged breath mirrored hers, and Ivy could see the lines of strain even in the gray light of dawn. But she didn't give in to the urge to touch him again. There was so much more distance between them than the couple of feet of bed. As she came down from the painful edge of arousal, she began to understand that he hadn't come fully back to himself when she kissed him. He hadn't come fully back until just now.

And the first thing he'd done was leap away from her as if she had leprosy.

The realization hollowed her out. A hot flush of humiliation swept over her, tightening her skin and making her stomach roil. None of it was enough to erase the imprint of his hands on her or the want still singing in her blood.

She grabbed a pillow to cover herself and waited to see what he'd say, braced herself for the apology and the declaration that this had been a mistake. Or maybe she was the one who should apologize. Apologize and hike out herself to escape this mortification.

In the end, Harrison said nothing. Shoving up from the bed, he grabbed his shirt, crossed to the narrow stairs and shimmied down them, never once making eye contact. Ivy could hear him moving around downstairs, putting on boots and going outside.

As the door shut, she let out a long, shuddering breath. That was not how she'd wanted that to go. Not that she'd expected her kiss to do anything but shock him out of whatever nightmare he'd been in.

Pulling her knees into her chest, she sat up. Maybe she should have realized sooner. But how could she? He'd wanted her, too. He wouldn't have kissed her like that, touched her like that, if he didn't. It had been her name he'd growled. Even if he hadn't been totally present, he'd still been seeing her. So why had he stopped? Maybe he thought he was taking advantage? If he'd bothered to ask... And why hadn't he asked? Why was his response to run away instead of to talk to her, ask her whether she was on the same page? She could've clarified that for him in a hurry, such that maybe at least one of them would've ended up satisfied this morning.

Nobody comes to a place like this if they want company.

Was he running? Hiding? Was there actually a difference?

Now, more than ever, she wanted to know the man inside the shell. And she wanted his kiss again.

HARRISON SUCKED in lungfuls of searing, winter air, hoping it would clear his head, wishing it would wipe away the sight of those bruises. But the image of those livid splashes of color against Ivy's pale skin was burned into his brain. Were any of them from him?

He scrubbed bare hands over his head. He'd worried about his inconvenient hard-on, copping a feel, not attacking her in his sleep. He'd been behind enemy lines; someone had tried to garrote him. He'd reacted, took control, neutralized the threat. Then the dream had inexplicably shifted to Ivy, warm and willing against him. And that was so much better than where he'd been, he'd rolled with it, giving in to all the urges to touch and taste and claim her. She was wet heat, lithe muscle under soft skin.

And then he woke up—because ripping off a woman's top will wake a guy up—and found himself all but mauling her, invading her space, with no memory of any kind of consent.

Christ, what could he say to her? How could he possibly apologize for putting his hands on her? He stared down at the broad expanse of them, knowing what they were capable of, what they'd done. He was a big guy, with a lot of training. She'd never be able to stop him if he didn't allow it, and he'd been too much in his head, too much in the dream to know for sure if she'd fought him. What if she had and he didn't notice?

The idea of it made him sick. He'd never in his life raised his hand to a woman, never taken advantage of one. Shame had his body flushing hot, beading with sweat despite the frigid temperatures. She'd trusted him and this was how he'd repaid her?

What if she was afraid of him?

If she was, he couldn't expect her to stay here alone with him. But the path to the Jeep was several inches deep in snow, and the driveway was entirely hidden. Even if temperatures rose enough today to melt the accumulation, getting up the incline to the road was going to be a challenge, and not necessarily safe. But if Ivy wanted to go, he'd figure something out. It was the least he could do.

Gathering up firewood, he vowed to give her whatever kind of space she needed. He went back inside, bracing himself to face her, half expecting her to be barricaded in the bathroom or backed into a corner with his combat knife. He wouldn't blame her.

But she was in the kitchen, dressed in jeans and some kind of belted sweater. Her hair was pulled back in a loose braid that draped over one shoulder as she gathered ingredients for breakfast. She glanced over, but said nothing as he crossed to the fireplace and began to methodically arrange logs over the ashes of last night's fire.

He needed to get this out fast. Like ripping off a Band-aid. "I'm sorry."

"It's fine." Her easy words pained him. Nothing about this was fine, and he didn't deserve the benefit of her brushing it under the rug.

"It's not fine, Ivy. I should never have put my hands on you. I had no right to touch you, no right to force myself on you." He bowed his head, wishing he could shrink himself.

"It can hardly be called force when I'm the one who kissed you first."

Shock had his head whipping up and around to face her. "What?"

She crossed her arms. "You were sleeping hard. You're a cover hog, by the way. I was trying to get some of the blankets back, and I guess I surprised you. You reacted to whatever you thought was happening and pinned me. You weren't responding to your name, so I kissed you to try to snap you out of it."

Harrison rewound events in his head. Maybe she hadn't been fighting him. Her legs had been wrapped around his hips, not as if she'd been trying to throw him off, but as if she'd wanted to pull him closer. He tried to summon up her face in that moment he'd awakened, tried to remember if there'd been fear. But all he could remember was lust. She'd seemed to be into things, into him.

Realizing that what he'd taken as a shift in dream had been reality, he closed his eyes, scrubbing a hand over his face. "And instead of sticking around and dealing with the situation directly, I freaked out and bolted." How must that have made her feel? "Jesus, Ivy, I'm so sorry. I've got no excuse." How could he admit he was this fucked-up half-man? "I—"

"Do I need to kiss you again to shut you up?"

Her irritated question stemmed the flow of words from his mouth. "What?"

She arched a brow. "Well, it worked the first time. Stop with the apologies and self-flagellation. You think you attacked me in your sleep, held me down, and molested me against my will. You didn't, and I'm not afraid of you. If anything, I'm the pervert for wrapping myself around you like kudzu when you weren't even awake."

"Honeysuckle."

"Huh?"

"You're honeysuckle, not kudzu, and definitely not a pervert." Relief that he wasn't a pervert either mingled with a regret for what might have been if he hadn't just reacted. "Whatever it was, I'm sorry I made it weird...er. Sorry I made it weirder."

"For the record, I liked kissing you. A lot. I liked having your hands on me. More than a lot. I wouldn't mind repeating both those things again."

His mouth had gone dry because it felt a helluva lot like she was giving him permission and his hands itched to pick back up where they'd left off. He shook his head, needing to put some distance between them so he didn't just leap over the couch to take her up on it. "Gotta be Stockholm Syndrome."

Ivy rolled her eyes. "It's not Stockholm Syndrome. It's forced cohabitation."

"It's what now?"

"Forced cohabitation is a well-loved fictional trope, in which two people are obligated to share living space, leading to all sorts of sexy shenanigans. I thought you were a reader."

"Maybe I need to get out of my comfort zone."

Her silver-green gaze was steady on his. "Maybe that's exactly what you need."

On that provocative pronouncement, she turned her back on him and retreated to the kitchen.

CHAPTER 8

*G*ood job, Ivy. If you needed further proof from the Universe that you made the right call not writing romance, this was it. And now you've made the remainder of our confinement together the most awkward thing ever.

What was she supposed to do now? Ignore the six-thousand pound gorilla in the room? The one with the "Crash and Burn" t-shirt, who was pointing and laughing?

Pretend nothing for the win. She'd been captaining the U.S.S. Denial for months now, so she ought to do just fine at that.

By the time he got the fire going again—it seemed to take Harrison about fifty times longer this morning. Because he was avoiding her? Nooo, why should she think that? In that time, she'd made a mountain of French toast and improvised a pour over system for some coffee because hell if she was going to face him again without it. For just a moment, she considered being really cowardly and petty and taking her breakfast up to the loft to eat alone. But other than the bathroom, there were no real walls in the whole cabin, so what point would that serve other than highlighting the division between them? Straightening her shoulders, she carried the platter of French toast to the table and set it for two. He'd either eat or he wouldn't. She wasn't going to let this breakfast go to waste.

Sitting down with her coffee, Ivy forked a couple of slices onto her plate. She could feel Harrison's eyes on her from the other side of the room. Irritation rose up to choke out the embarrassment, but she didn't give it voice. This was on her. She was the one who'd made it weird. *"For the record..."* Ugh! If she was anything other than relaxed and normal, it would exacerbate this awkwardness between them, and it was already as big as the Statue of Liberty.

"Come eat while it's hot."

He crossed the room with far less noise than a man of his size ought to make. With no more fanfare, he dropped into the chair across from her, his gaze flickering to her face and back to the food.

"Looks good."

"I made too much. But the leftovers should reheat okay in the oven later."

He loaded his own plate and they ate, silence descending again. Ivy kept her focus on the food and on the life-giving beverage she'd managed to brew. Coffee—even weird, MacGuyver-brewed coffee—made everything better. As the caffeine hit her system, she tried to set aside her discomfort to get a better read on him. But she couldn't quite manage anything longer than quick glances in his direction, all of which showed him eating with a single-minded focus that probably spoke more of his inclination to avoid the awkward than the superiority of her cooking. She hated that their camaraderie had been ruined and wondered if she should just bring up the possibility of heading into town today as soon as conditions would allow.

"I had an idea about how to maybe fix your plot problem."

Jerked from her thoughts, Ivy lifted her gaze to Harrision's. "What?"

"You said they wanted a spinoff series with Michael, right?"

So they were going to talk about her books now? Okay, she'd take that olive branch. "Yeah."

"But he's not that interesting on his own. He's too closed off. We know he's been through some shit—all of them have—but he gives off this air of having dealt with all of his. That doesn't make him compelling as a character we want to follow for several more books."

"He's boring." Maybe she should've been offended by his assessment, but she couldn't disagree with it.

"Not boring. Just not the obvious choice because we don't see where his character arc would take him. We don't see how he might change or what he needs to learn."

Ivy put down her fork and wrapped both hands around the lingering warmth of her mug as her brain latched onto the problem. "*Yes.* I've gone rounds with Michael, trying to figure out what the hell his goal is, what he's motivated by, and getting nowhere. Because he really doesn't have one. Not like Sloan. He's not a team player. It was why he left."

The awkwardness faded as Harrison's eyes snapped with interest. "Was it? Or was it because there was someone else on the team that reminded him of old wounds? Someone who's been where he's been, who went through the same kind of dark shit but hasn't made it out. Someone he doesn't want to give enough of a damn about to peel back some of that armor and revisit his own pain in the name of helping her find her way."

"Her? You're talking about Annika?"

He nodded. "I think Michael really left because he couldn't handle being around her. Because her shit—whatever it is—hit too close to home. And he got through his by not letting himself care. By hardening himself. She challenged that, just by being in the same space with him. So what better way to introduce conflict than to put the two of them together on some long-term mission or case where they can't escape each other because that's the job?"

Were they still just talking about her book? Ivy wasn't sure.

But she considered. "He needs a proper foil. The protagonists always do, but in the past I've always used the antagonist for that. It hadn't occurred to me to use somebody considered one of the good guys."

"Part of why your characters are so interesting is that they aren't all good or all evil. They're complex. Annika is volatile. She's entirely in control—until she's not. You've never gotten into the why of that, and as a reader I always wondered what her secret was. She's never said—or I guess you haven't—but there was always that intimation that she'd done something that made her question whether she *was* one of the good guys. That her real motivation for being on the team was to earn redemption for... whatever that thing is she won't tell anybody."

Ivy didn't admit to him that Annika had kept her secret because she as the author didn't know what it was. It hadn't been relevant to the book she'd appeared in, so Ivy hadn't delved any deeper. She wasn't sure she should now.

But Harrison saw something in her character. He'd spoken of redemption, of Annika wondering whether she was one of the good guys. Was he projecting?

Ivy considered what she knew of him, both what he'd told her and what she'd surmised. He'd been Special Forces, out of the military for a few years. He'd said himself he'd come here to escape something and she was a welcome distraction. She'd seen first-hand that he could still get lost in the past. He'd all but fallen all over himself to apologize when he thought he might have hurt or taken advantage of her in that state. His streak of honor was wide and obvious, yet he wasn't willing to acknowledge it. He hadn't wanted thanks or praise for her rescue, and clearly he didn't see himself as a hero.

She suspected he'd lost someone on his team or under his command. Maybe both. Didn't matter whether it was bad intel or an accident or just the realities of battle. He was the kind who'd blame himself either way. That would be a helluva thing to carry and a logical reason for why he'd cut himself off. He didn't trust himself to be responsible for anyone else. And maybe, just maybe, his failure to respond to her had more to do with not believing he deserved anything good in his life than with general horror over her forward behavior.

So how could she help him see he was wrong?

"The secret Annika's been guarding so fiercely, that would have to come out over the course of the series, is about how her last squad died. She's carrying all this survivor's guilt, and it's slowly killing her. What she'd have to learn as the series progressed, is that shit happens. Especially in war. There was nothing she could have done, and it wasn't her fault."

"How will she figure that out?" Harrison's voice cracked a little, and he seemed surprised he'd even asked the question.

That alone let her know she was on the right track in her assessment, so she chose her next words with care, trying to figure out what it was he needed to hear. "I don't know yet. But maybe the new team would help. Maybe Michael would help. Because, you're right, he's dealt with his issues. He'd be a good, prospective wayfinder for her, if she'd open herself up to listen to whatever he'll share. But being off on her own, closing herself off from life, hasn't helped. The alternative is that she looks at the opportunities she's presented with and actively chooses life, chooses to engage, chooses to feel."

His throat worked and those dark eyes were fixed on hers with an expression she couldn't quite read. "Even if feeling is what makes her reckless?"

Ivy wondered again if he was still talking about the book. "Feeling isn't what makes her reckless. It's not *letting* herself feel. Because closing herself off gives all of it a chance to fester rather than bleed free. It's that build-up that drives her outbursts." Even as she said it, she knew it was true. Of Annika, and probably of Harrison, too.

"Some hurts can be packed away and forgotten about, and

they'll fade with time. And some become caged animals that do more damage, become more feral, the longer they're ignored. She'll have to eventually bring it out into the light and work with it to work through it to have any chance at being whole again."

Her brain sputtered with the first sparks of creativity she'd felt in ages, and she began to see how it could be. Annika would challenge Michael, and he, in turn, would settle her. They'd be more together than alone...

"Maybe she'll never be whole again." His voice was gravel as he spoke and the haunted expression in his eyes touched her deeper than the physical ever could.

They definitely weren't talking about Annika now, so she shoved aside the stirrings of plot to focus on him. "She won't know until she tries." Ivy wanted to reach out and touch him, as a show of support, of human connection. But she didn't know how he'd respond if she broke out of the metaphor of the book. This was his truth, his burden, and it was intensely personal.

His long, dark lashes swept down, shutting away his thoughts. When he opened his eyes again, he'd locked down whatever emotion their discussion had stirred up. "Well, then, seems like you've got to give her a mission that will get her over her initial resistance."

Sensing Harrison had reached some kind of limit, Ivy turned her mind back to the book and to the scrap of notes she'd dictated, where Annika had been the one to go after Michael for recruitment. Maybe there'd been something buried in her subconscious about this in the first place. Her brain turned over the new pieces, using Annika as the lens instead of Michael himself—and her brain finally began to fire. She felt like writing for the first time in forever.

"I think you just might be onto something."

The corners of Harrison's mouth tipped up in the barest of smiles as he pushed back from the table. "Go write while it's cooking. I'm gonna go try to sort out the generator."

This time, when he retreated, it didn't feel like he wanted to shut her out. It seemed like a natural pause to breathe for them both. Maybe they would be okay. And maybe, before their time together was through, she'd help him find his way to the answers he needed.

With that in mind, she opened her laptop and began to type.

HARRISON MADE his way through the snow to the lean-to, still reeling. He'd intended that conversation to just be brainstorming. A way for them to get back to some kind of even keel before they talked about what came next—which he'd still expected to be *When can you get me out of here?* But the whole thing had turned intensely personal. He had no one to blame for that but himself. He was the one pushing Annika as a character. He'd done it because he knew what that volatile state was like. He'd lived it for his first two years out of the Army. Was, apparently, still living it. As a reader, he wanted to see Annika get to the other side because he needed the same answers she did.

"The secret Annika's been guarding so fiercely is about how her last squad died. She's carrying all this survivor's guilt, and it's slowly killing her. What she'll have to learn is that shit happens. Especially in war. There was nothing she could have done, and it wasn't her fault."

As he worked his way through troubleshooting the generator, he wondered if that really was Annika's secret. Or was Ivy the profiler reading him like one of her books? Survivor's guilt was a reality in the military. People died in war. Those who were left behind were doomed to struggle with it. People like Ty. Like himself. The weight of those memories, that one decision, had been what drove him up here. Setting him on Ivy's path. He didn't believe in fate. He'd seen too damned much that defied any kind of preordination. And yet here she was, reaching out to offer that connection, that advice that cutting himself off wasn't helping.

Well, it had been advice for Annika, but he didn't think either of them had been talking about her at the end.

Harrison wasn't sure what to do with that.

Realizing the generator wasn't getting fuel, he trudged back to his Jeep to retrieve some tools. The morning sky was overcast, and he was willing to bet there was more snow in those clouds. Which meant they probably weren't going anywhere. Not easily. Either way, it would probably be a while before normal power was restored, so he needed to get the generator working for himself, if nothing else. He'd take the fuel pump apart and see if it was just trash in the lines or if the thing had actually gone bad. If it was busted, maybe he could pick up another one in town when he took Ivy in.

He should have mentioned getting her back to town, made some kind of offer to try, or at least apologized that he couldn't. He just didn't want to bring it up. And how selfish was that? One way or another, he was the one who'd screwed up this morning. Not only did he let her share the blame, but when she all but said, "Let's try that again," he'd just left her hanging there. He had good reason to keep his hands off her. He was a bad bet. But he could have said that, instead of...nothing.

I can't do any damned thing right.

Small wonder. He was broken. He'd known that for a long time now.

"Some hurts can be packed away and forgotten about, and they'll fade with time. And some become caged animals that do more damage, become more feral, the longer they're ignored. She'll have to eventually bring it out into the light and work with it to work through it to have any chance at being whole again."

He thought he'd done that. Pouring out all those memories into fiction, where he explored the million and one what-if scenarios that had plagued him the past three years. And what would Ivy say if he told her he was a writer, too? He wasn't anywhere near the level she was, but his self-published military science fiction had found a niche following and earned some minor acclaim. Maybe more surprising, it had given him an unexpected living and the freedom to borrow a friend's cabin just to sulk for a week. But it wasn't exorcising those demons. He'd just been reliving them over and over—with lasers and cool, space tech. He'd thought he'd worked through more of it, but Garrett's funeral and seeing Ty ripping himself to shreds with guilt just brought everything back to the surface.

So what was the answer?

Clearing the debris out of the fuel line, he began to reassemble the fuel pump.

"The alternative is that she looks at the opportunities she's presented with and actively chooses life, chooses to engage, chooses to feel."

What the hell did that even look like? Did it really mean choosing to forge some real connection with Ivy? Taking her up on her offer?

God, his hands itched to touch her again, to fill his palms with her breasts and feel the heat of her pressed against him. The blood drained into his lap as he imagined finishing what they'd started, stripping her bare so he could taste every inch of her before burying himself in all that wet heat.

The screws slipped out of his hand. Swearing, he bent over to dig through the snow for them.

He needed to slow his roll. Not that he didn't believe she wanted him. She'd made that clear enough. But was choosing her, choosing intimacy—he wasn't under any delusion after that talk that being with her would be just sex—actually a step in the right direction? Or was it more distraction from the essential pain of living?

Did it matter? He wanted her. She wanted him. That should be simple math. But he suspected nothing with Ivy would be simple.

He reinstalled the fuel pump without further mishap. One, two, three cranks and the motor roared to life. Well, at least he knew how to fix some things.

Putting away his tools, Harrison went back inside, dreading the inevitable question of when he could take her back into town so she could get back to the getaway she'd actually planned.

Ivy sat in the chair by the fire, fingers flying over the laptop balanced on her legs. Immersed in whatever she was working on, she didn't even seem to notice him. She was in the zone. Absurdly relieved he didn't have to face the issue of town—yet, anyway—he left her to it, using the time to clean up so he didn't smell like gas.

She was still head down when he came back out. A few locks of hair had escaped the messy bun to brush at her cheek, but she didn't seem to notice as her fingers flew over the keys. He had a feeling a bomb could go off nearby and she wouldn't register a thing. Feeling a sense of kinship, his lips tugged into a smile. He understood what that level of immersion meant for her, for her career—maybe more for her mental health. The dam had been broken and now she needed to ride the wave of creativity as far as it would take her.

Fly, little bird, fly.

He wanted to keep her here. To protect this little oasis for her where she couldn't or wouldn't do it for herself.

Right. Because it's entirely about her and not because the moment she walks out of your life, everything's going back to being gray.

Uncomfortable with the thought and realizing he was just kind of staring at her, he moved quietly to the kitchen. He'd just make a pot of coffee and settle in with a book.

Ivy didn't stir until he set a mug on the little table by her chair. Her nose twitched, her head popping up. "Coffee?"

Her hopeful tone made him smile. "I thought you might want another cup."

Losing some of that glazed expression, she came fully back to the present. "We have power!"

"We do. I take it the book or outline or whatever is going well?"

She set the laptop on the coffee table and rose, wincing a little as she unfolded her legs. "It is! I have a *plot,* Harrison. An actual, honest-to-goodness, not-total-piece-of-steaming-crap plot. Or most of one anyway. I've got all my major plot points, and a helluva start on both character arcs."

"Both?"

Her words spilled out in a frantic, enthusiastic rush. "I have to tell Annika's story alongside Michael's. Because they're inextricably intertwined. I didn't see it before. I had him out there on his own and I wasn't getting anywhere, but now I am. She needs him. And he'll change for her. She's the only one it could be, and I finally see it because of *you,* you brilliant man." Eyes gleaming with excitement, she bounced up, throwing her arms around his neck and pressing a smacking kiss to his mouth.

It was fast, friendly, and she pulled back almost at once. But it was enough for the taste of her to hit him like a drug. Color heated her cheeks and distress dimmed those silver-green eyes.

He hated it. Hated that she felt a moment of discomfort over sharing her excitement. Hated that he'd done anything to bring her down from that creative high.

"I'm sorry. I didn't mean..." She trailed off as he slid a hand into her hair.

"No, I'm sorry." He skimmed a thumb over her bottom lip and watched the distress melt into confused arousal. "I screwed this up. But I can do better. Will do better, if you'll let me." Stepping into her, he lowered his mouth until it was a breath away from hers. "Tell me to stop, and I'll stop."

"Don't." Her whispered reply feathered over his lips and he was lost to do anything but close that last finite distance.

CHAPTER 9

*I*vy's tiny gasp and sigh sparked a fire in Harrison's blood.

He didn't remember kissing her this morning. Not really. He'd been too much in his head, still partly dreaming. But he would remember this. The gradual surrender as she melted into him, her hands curling into the front of his shirt, the silk of her hair in his fingers.

He wanted her to remember it, too, so he took his time, exploring her lips and drinking in every little nuance. As he traced the seam of her mouth, she opened for him, instantly angling her head for a deeper kiss. Her ready acquiescence had his patience straining, but he continued to sip, to savor, steeping himself in the taste of her. She was so sweet, so...open. He could get drunk on kissing her alone.

The pulse in her throat hammered against his thumb, urging his own heartbeat into a gallop. But still, he held himself in check. If they were going to do this, he was going to take his time. He'd make it good for her. Make it worth her taking this chance on him.

Rising to her toes, Ivy pressed more firmly against him. His erection nudged her belly. She was short. Too short for them to easily line up while standing. Blindly, he backed them toward the sofa, praying he didn't run into the table and upset the coffee. Abruptly bumping into the sofa, he sat down hard, breaking their kiss. Ivy followed him down, finding his mouth again like a heat-seeking missile as she straddled his lap, fitting herself against the bulge in his jeans.

Harrison groaned, skimming his hands up her back and into her hair.

"Too many clothes," she complained.

"Working on it." His hands went to the belt of her sweater, tugging the knot free.

With considerably less patience, she shoved his flannel shirt off his shoulders, growling a little when it caught. The sound shot straight to his cock. He couldn't stop himself from holding her close and bucking against her heat, torturing them both. Her tongue dipped into his mouth, even as she tugged up his t-shirt, seeking skin. More than happy to oblige, he broke the kiss, yanking the shirt up and off.

Ivy's pupils all but swallowed up the green of her eyes as she took in the sight of him. She sucked in a slow breath. "I didn't have adequate opportunity to appreciate this earlier." She trailed a finger down his shoulder, over one pec to circle his nipple. "God was in a very, very good mood when He made you."

"Pretty sure that was the United States Army."

"God bless America." Her mouth came back to his, unabashedly greedy as her hands streaked over his chest and shoulders.

He loved every second.

Tunneling beneath her shirt, he stroked his fingers over her back, her ribs, and higher to cup her breasts. On a moan, Ivy arched into the touch, her nipples pearling. He wanted to taste them, wanted to see them but contented himself for the moment with exploring by touch, seeing how she responded when he tugged down the cups of her bra and skimmed his roughened fingers over her tender skin.

"More. Very definitely more of that." As if to help him along with that decision, she grasped the hem of her shirt and tugged it off.

The sight of the livid bruising slapped him in the face again. It ran from her left shoulder down to her right hip, clearly showing where she'd been thrown against the seat belt. His hands stilled. She'd been in an accident just yesterday. What the hell was he doing?

Ivy cupped his face in her hand, forcing his gaze up. "It looks worse than it is. It doesn't hurt."

He'd been bruised countless times, in countless ways. He knew the stages, knew the level of pain associated with each. There was no way in hell this didn't hurt.

"Please don't stop."

She wanted this, wanted him, and God knew, he wanted her. So he wouldn't stop, but he'd damned well find some control and finesse and be gentle about it.

Leaning forward, Harrison pressed a soft kiss to her shoulder, where the angry purple began. Ivy's breath hitched, her fingers spearing into his hair to hold him to her. He traced the path of the bruising with his mouth.

"I was never a fan of the whole kiss it make it better thing, but you're changing my mind."

He smiled against her skin, taking a moment to linger between her breasts as he unfastened her bra and drew it off. He traced the inner curve of each breast with his tongue, wanting more, needing more, but holding himself back. He had a mission to complete now—to make her forget she'd been injured at all.

Lifting his head, he combed his fingers through her thick, brown hair. "Let's go upstairs."

She slid off his lap, sending him a heated look over her shoulder as she crossed the room. Harrison thought he'd happily follow her anywhere. He admired the sway of her ass as she preceded him up the steep, narrow staircase, and maybe that was how he missed when her nerves crept back in.

As he stepped into the loft, he saw her deliberately unclench her fingers and straighten rounded shoulders, a quick flash of uncertainty giving way to relief. The realization that she'd thought he might change his mind and turn away from her again was a punch to the gut.

Jesus, he'd been a jackass.

Wanting to put her at ease again, he framed her face and kissed her, long and deep, until she relaxed against him, her arms snaking around his waist.

"Still okay?"

"Why aren't we naked yet?" Ah, there was that sweet tone of demand again.

His lips kicked up. "You in a hurry?"

"Kinda."

"Too bad. I'm not." Determined to make up for giving her any reason to doubt him, he drowned the protest she made with another kiss designed to make her forget exactly what she was complaining about.

Nudging her back on the bed, Harrison efficiently pulled off her shoes and socks. Instead of starting in on her jeans, he crawled up the bed, up her body, close enough that the hair of his chest brushed against the sensitive skin of her breasts. Her breath hitched and she arched into him. And didn't that just put her long, lovely neck right there for his mouth to feast on?

Ivy tipped her head back as he began to explore the side of her throat. "More skin-to-skin."

Harrison had been a soldier for a lot of years. He knew how to take orders. He dragged his stubbled cheek across her collar bone. "I intend to taste every inch of your skin. Does that work for you?"

Ivy's entire body clenched beneath him in anticipation. "Given what your mouth is doing to me so far, I suspect it absolutely will. But just so you know, I really want to feel your hands again."

He didn't often have cause to think about his hands in a positive light. The things he'd done with them in the line of duty—Harrison cut off the thought, glancing up to where they circled her wrists, pinning her loosely in place. If she liked the idea of his hands, he was more than happy to put them to better use. "Where?"

"Everywhere," she breathed.

Oh yeah, he could get into that. "How about we do both?"

"Please, God, yes."

He used them on her—fingers, tongue, teeth, lips—until every exposed inch quivered with need and sensation. She encouraged him every step of the way, saying exactly what she liked, what she loved, what she needed more of. Then, and only then, did he strip off her jeans and panties to continue his thorough exploration, working his way up her legs from her delicate ankles.

As he began to nuzzle the soft, soft skin at the inside of her thigh, Ivy muttered, "I might simply burn up and die if you don't hurry up and put that mouth where I need it most."

Smiling again—he'd smiled more since this woman came into his life than the entire past year—he asked, "Do you always talk this much during sex?"

"What?" The word came out strained.

"You've had this kind of one-sided dialogue going since we got started up here."

"I have?"

"Mmm." He kissed a couple inches higher.

Her body tensed. "I used to be a sleep talker as a kid. I didn't know I was a sex talker."

Sorry he'd inadvertently embarrassed her, he gently pressed apart the knees she'd begun to close so he could look up the length of her body into her eyes. "I love knowing what I'm doing to you."

The vulnerability on her face had little to do with his position between her legs. "You do?"

"It's incredibly fucking hot. And, for the record, you won't die. Not on my watch."

"Good to knooo—oh *God.*"

At the first touch of his tongue down her center, she bowed up off the bed, hands fisting in the covers. He simply used his hands to hold her hips steady as he began to lick and suck at her most sensitive flesh, until the only word she could manage was his name. She screamed it as the orgasm ripped through her.

Best sound ever.

As she lay gasping for breath, Harrison prowled up her body again, reaching for one of the condoms in his wallet on the bedside table.

"You lied." Because the words sounded conversational instead of accusatory, he didn't slow his movements.

"About what?"

"I really don't think I just lived through that. It was too good. Glad I went out on a high note, though."

This woman was good for his ego.

On a chuckle, Harrison rose over her, loving her flushed, sated look in the middle of the rumpled bed and knowing he'd done that. "You're quite the soprano, but I expect we can find proof of life yet." He stroked the blunt tip of his cock through the wetness between her thighs.

Already arching up to him, Ivy levered up to brush her lips over his. "I do appreciate a man who loves a challenge."

Harrison followed her mouth back down, covering her body with his as he eased inside her. Wrapping her legs around his hips, she dug her heels into his ass, urging him deeper.

Christ almighty, she felt so good.

And she was suddenly too quiet. Shit. "You stopped talking. You okay? Did I hurt you?"

Ivy framed his face, eyes searching his for...what?

He couldn't stop himself from cupping her cheek, wanting to do something, anything to reassure her. She shouldn't ever have cause to doubt him again.

Evidently finding what she needed, she offered the sweetest smile as she tipped her mouth up to his. "So very okay."

He'd make sure she stayed that way. He began to move in a torturously slow, controlled rhythm that had her body coiling again for the climb. He was climbing with her this time, drawing on every shred of control he possessed not to simply plunge into her and lose himself. Because she was better for him than her books, better than writing. Right here, with her, he couldn't think of anything but the slow, blistering glide of their bodies coming together.

Her hands streaked over him, fraying his control as she met him thrust for thrust. As she neared the edge, her body beginning to ripple around him, he fought to hang on, to put her first.

"Harrison."

His gaze sharpened on hers. She looked up at him, seemingly into him, and he felt more exposed than he ever had in his life. But what shields could he have here, buried inside her? Did she see that he was broken? That he didn't deserve this? Didn't deserve her?

He faltered.

Her hands curled into his shoulders. "With me. Come with me."

At her demand, he dropped his brow to hers. "Ivy."

"With me," she repeated, her climax already gripping him. "Let go. You can let go."

And like the good soldier he'd been, he followed orders.

～

EVERY SINGLE ONE of Ivy's nerve endings was alight. If she opened her eyes, she was positive she'd be glowing. She'd have to check.

In a minute. Or twenty. Her limbs felt heavy. So did Harrison's weight stretched out on her, though he'd tucked his arms alongside her torso to keep from crushing her.

"I'll move in a minute." His voice rumbled against the crook of her neck.

Because her hand was conveniently already there, Ivy stroked it through the hair at his nape, enjoying the slide of the strands through her fingers. "No rush. You make an excellent blanket."

They lay there, still joined, breathing together in the silence. Ivy waited for that to feel strange. Instead it felt...peaceful, as if they'd done this countless times before. Her life would definitely be richer if they had, and she had high hopes that they would do it again. Preferably as soon as he was physically able. And maybe sometime later. Or a lot of times later. She was really beginning to see the benefits of a blizzard.

Harrison stirred, pushing himself up enough to look down at her. He held there for a long moment, and Ivy felt the weight of his stare down to her bones.

"I'll be right back." He rolled off and went to take care of the essentials.

Ivy stared at the ceiling, her throat dry. This whole encounter was more than she'd bargained for. Beyond the mind-numbing pleasure—and holy shit, he was amazing—there was a gravity to what they'd just done that shook her. Everything about him had been so wholly unexpected and she didn't know exactly what to do about it. About them. If there was a them.

He came back up the stairs, bottled waters in hand. Twisting the cap off one, he handed it over.

Ivy guzzled down half.

"I really hope you were at a good stopping point in the outline," he said, sipping at his own bottle. "Because I'm not letting you out of this bed."

As threats went, it was one she could absolutely get behind. Her body hummed at the erotic glint in his eyes. His shields were up again. Apparently, he was intent on ignoring the weight of this thing between them. He knew it was there. She'd seen it in his face, unguarded as they'd made love—because nothing about what they'd done had been just sex. But he wasn't ready to meet her there yet. This was more than she'd expected, more than she'd planned, as he was more. So she wouldn't make the mistake she'd made before of sharing her observations too soon.

Because it was what he seemed to want, she dug deep to find some levity. She met his gaze over the bottle. "This whole interlude gives 'Thank you for your service' a whole new meaning. I don't think I've ever been serviced quite so well."

He snorted out a laugh and flopped into bed beside her. "Happy to oblige." The hand he laid high on her thigh told her he'd be happy to oblige again. "So *were* you at a good stopping point in your outline?"

She finished off the water and set the bottle to the side, intent on freeing her hands to touch him again. "Good enough. I poured out the lion's share of that first rush. I can't believe I didn't see it before, how they'd fit together."

Her gaze traced the coat of arms tattoo on his biceps. She hadn't really noticed it before. The shield held a sun, a star, and a lightning bolt and told her without a word that he was an Airborne Ranger, part of the Army's seventy-fifth regiment. Special Forces. No wonder he hadn't thought a thing about rappelling down a snowy mountainside.

"I thought you didn't write romance."

"Not as a focus, but relationships add stakes and depth to a story, not to mention verisimilitude and a great vehicle for change. Seeing a closed off character open up because of love is incredibly satisfying as a reader. I don't think either of them will have the necessary vulnerability to impact each other without it. And I think you were exactly right. Michael is afraid of caring about her, of what he'd do for her."

The hand on her thigh clenched for just a moment before

relaxing. "There's not much more than love that'll send a man straight into hell. Whether it's love of a woman or love of a brother."

She wondered what hell he'd walked through and for whom.

Laying a hand on his chest, Ivy trailed her fingers over the ridges and planes, gratified at the way his breath quickened. Several scars added character to that beautiful body. She didn't avoid them, but didn't pay any undue attention either. She had no trouble imagining a knife fight or Harrison hunkered down with his men, taking fire from insurgents. But she wouldn't ask him about any of that. Not now. Still, her curiosity was more than piqued. They'd been as intimate as two people could be, but she still knew next to nothing about him.

"Tell me something real about you."

"Something real?"

"Yeah. Like—I don't know—what was your first car? The name of your dog growing up? When did you lose your virginity?"

"An '88 Oldsmobile, Buster, and Mandy Gilcrest, in the back of that Oldsmobile on graduation night."

"I suppose a land yacht would be handy for backseat space. My granddaddy had one of those. That thing was freaking *huge*. You could fit a whole side of beef in the trunk."

"They don't make 'em like that anymore, that's for sure." His tone held the kind of affection only men seemed to hold for vehicles.

Okay, she really didn't want to talk about cars. She wanted to talk about him. "Tell me something else."

His fingers traced patterns on her back. "Just ask."

A hundred questions leapt to her lips, but she held them back. She didn't want to ruin this by voicing any of the ones she really wanted to know. "Where did you grow up?"

"Little town in Washington, near the coast. What about you?"

"Well, as I said, I was a preacher's kid, so we moved a lot. Most of my childhood was in South Alabama at varying distances from Mobile. Mom, Dad, sister."

"You're the oldest."

"I'm the oldest," she confirmed.

Leaning up, she pressed a soft kiss to the scar on his cheek. "What's this really from?"

"Coffee mug. It was Mother's Day and I was six. I'd made her breakfast. Which was really a bowl of cereal with an orange. But I'd watched her make coffee every day of my life, so I made some of that. Probably got the ratio of grounds to water all kinds of wrong, but I was so damned proud I'd managed the machine. I was in a rush, trying to get it all done before she woke up, so I could surprise her, and I tripped as I was carrying it to the tray on the kitchen table. The mug crashed to the floor and I hit right after. Landed right on one of the pieces of the mug. So instead of the nice relaxing morning I'd planned for her, we spent it in the ER getting stitches."

But he'd tried. She liked knowing that even when he was little, he'd tried to do something to take care of his mom. She liked, too, that not all of his scars were from his military service.

"Y'all are tight?"

"Yeah. It was just us growing up." He didn't elaborate and Ivy didn't press.

Because she wasn't sure she could hold back the rest of the questions she wanted to ask and because she didn't want to screw this up, Ivy decided the best course of action for them both was distraction. Sitting up, she swung a leg over his and shifted to straddle him. "Are you done with your water?"

Arching a brow, he drained the last of his bottle and tossed it.

"Good. Because as my current muse, I think I should get to study this body for research, and round one was all about you studying mine."

He grinned and sat up, running his hands down her back. "It's my new favorite subject."

The position made it more than clear he'd had enough time to recover. Digging for some control, she shoved him back. Or tried. He didn't budge an inch. "Lay back down and be a good test subject so I can take some notes. With my mouth."

Harrison dropped back, arms spread wide. "Yes, ma'am."

CHAPTER 10

They made love and talked and made love again until eventually starvation drove them to the kitchen, where they devoured the leftover French toast, still cold, before hitting the shower, where they had each other again. With each kiss, each caress, each climax, Harrison felt a few more layers of armor peel back—his and hers. They spoke of everything and nothing. Ivy told him about her childhood, of moving often, just when she'd really settled into a place.

"It made me rootless, I guess." She sprawled in his lap after their shower, wearing nothing but his shirt and a satisfied smile, her fingers tracing patterns on his nape.

Harrison stroked the wet hair back from her face. "Wouldn't your family have been your roots?"

"I mean, they were. They did their best. But I'll never get to go 'home' for holidays. I don't have one house I grew up in with all these built-up memories. I don't really have childhood best friends that I stayed close to. I learned never to get attached to places—or people either, really. I had to learn to appreciate the moment."

Was that what this was for her? Was that why she was able to throw herself into an unplanned affair with such enthusiasm? Harrison didn't like the idea that she already had her eye on the end of things. He hadn't been looking for this, hadn't planned for it, but he couldn't imagine walking away from her after today and never seeing her again. He didn't know exactly what this was beyond the first real connection he'd felt in years, but he wasn't ready to let her go. And that scared the shit out of him.

He tightened his arms around her and opened his mouth to say—he didn't know what. But his undoubtedly ill-advised honesty was interrupted by a knock on the door.

Ivy tensed. "Expecting someone?"

"No. No one knows I'm here except my friend, Porter. It's his cabin." But surely he hadn't come all the way out here in all this snow. Unless it had melted while they were otherwise occupied? He slid Ivy off his lap and buttoned his jeans.

Though no one could see in through the blinds, she tugged down the tails of his flannel shirt. "I'm just gonna zip up to the loft and get pants."

Harrison scooped up his discarded t-shirt and waited until she'd disappeared behind the half-wall to open the door. This was gonna be fun to explain to his buddy.

But it wasn't Porter on the porch. A broad-shouldered guy with a badge pinned to his thick winter coat stood in the doorway. "Harrison Wilkes?"

He shifted his weight, instinctively blocking the man's view inside. "Yeah?"

"I'm Sheriff Xander Kincaid. A friend of Porter's. He asked me to check on you since I was doing patrols on this side of the county."

"Oh." Harrison relaxed a notch. "Well, I'm fine. I've got the generator going and plenty of supplies."

"He'll be relieved to know you made it okay. Not everybody did. We had a guest expected at the inn in town. It's looking like she went over the side a little over a mile from here. One of my deputies is waiting on some of our search and rescue guys to go down and check the wreckage, but we don't have a lot of hope, not after how cold it got last night." The other man's face was set in preparation for facing the grim reality of body retrieval.

"Chevy Blazer?"

The sheriff's eyes sharpened. "Yeah. Did you see something on your way up here?"

Harrison glanced back at the loft, where Ivy was making her way down the narrow staircase. "I'm happy to report you won't be notifying any next of kin. The driver's right here." He stepped back, opening the door fully.

Xander stepped inside, going brows up as he caught sight of Ivy, who still wore Harrison's flannel shirt. "Ivy Blake?"

"Guilty. I take it you found my truck."

"Yeah, just a bit ago. I—" His gaze skimmed over her in quick assessment. "You weren't hurt?"

Ivy lifted a hand to the cut on her temple. "Not badly. A few scrapes. Some bruises. Harrison found me about an hour after I went through the rail. He's the one who got me out."

The sheriff's gaze swung to him. "By yourself?"

Harrison shrugged. "Nobody else around at the time."

"Damn. Let me just say we're all glad you came by. And you, Miss Blake, are a very lucky woman to have made it out of that wreck alive and in one piece. Pru will be so relieved. She was worried sick when you didn't show yesterday."

"Pru?" Harrison asked.

"My sister-in-law. She and her husband and my wife run The Misfit Inn where Miss Blake has reservations."

"I'm sorry about not calling. My phone was toast in the wreck, the cabin doesn't have a phone, and we haven't ventured out in the snow to try to find a signal."

Xander turned back to Ivy. "It's spotty around here anyway. Listen, I'm not sure what we can do about your vehicle before everything thaws, but I can take you back into town, drop you at the inn. The local doctor will absolutely come by to check you out."

Harrison bit back the urge to say she was fine exactly where she was. All day they'd avoided the topic of going into town. But this was it—the big intrusion of the outside world. Their intimate little bubble had been broken.

His mind raced, trying to figure out some way to suggest she stay with him. For all he'd thought he wanted to be alone, he'd found he didn't. He wanted to be with her. She'd proved to be a better distraction from his shit than anything else. Not just because of the sex—though that was fantastic—but just because of...her. She kept him in the now, pulled him back when he began to slip. And beyond all that, he'd enjoyed the hell out of her company. She was interesting. Working with her brainstorming her plot was the most legitimate fun he'd had in ages. He wanted to tell her about his own work and maybe talk through what it was he needed to do with his own plot problems. Was it weird that he'd waited this long to bring it up?

Despite all of it, he didn't speak. It wasn't fair of him to ask her to stay. She'd had a plan before the wreck interrupted it. She had a life she probably needed to get back to, details to sort out. Hell, there were probably other people she really should call to notify that she was okay. He was...just a break. A distraction for her. That was all they could be to each other.

"Actually, Sheriff, if it's all the same to you, I think I'll stay here. Harrison and I were going to go into town later on, once the roads were more clear, so I can take care of some business."

She wanted to stay. Here. With him. Relief had the tension draining out of his muscles so fast he dropped back to lean against the arm of the sofa. He crossed his arms as if he'd done it on purpose.

Xander divided a speculative look between them. "If you're sure."

Ivy's lips curved into an easy smile. "I'm sure."

"All right. I'll let Pru know."

Harrison followed Xander to the door. "If you'll just tell Porter I'll be in touch next time I make it to town?"

"Sure can. Y'all take care." With one last look at Ivy, the sheriff nodded and headed out.

Harrison stood at the window, watching him back a big ass Bronco up the drive. The tires slipped and slid a little in the snow, but he made it onto the road with less trouble than Harrison would've expected. Over the course of the day, it appeared the snow had finally stopped. But for the fresh tracks behind his Jeep, nothing interrupted their winter wonderland.

"Harrison?"

He swung around. "Yeah?"

The casual smile she'd shot at Xander was gone. She rolled her bottom lip between her teeth. "I shouldn't have sent him off without actually talking to you first. Is this really okay? Me staying? I mean, I made an assumption after—" She waved a hand between the two of them. "But you know what they say about assumptions."

Wanting to put her at ease, he crossed the room sliding his arms around her. "It's so okay." He dropped a quick, soft kiss to her lips before resting his brow against hers. "I wanted you to stay. But I couldn't figure out how to ask without putting you on the spot."

Her face brightened. "Really?"

"Really." He laced his fingers at the small of her back and grinned. "How else am I gonna find out how Annika and Michael get together before anybody else?"

She tugged back just enough to look him in the face with narrowed, laughing eyes. "Harrison Wilkes, are you a closet romantic?"

He didn't know, but this woman had sure as hell made his heart start beating again. And he was pretty sure he liked it.

~

"I DON'T WANNA." Ivy grimaced at the new, pre-paid cell phone she'd picked up at the little general store.

Across the table of their booth in Crystal's Diner, Harrison picked up his grilled mac and cheese sandwich. "You can't avoid her forever."

"I don't know. I feel like you know all about how to go off the grid. You could help me disappear." He'd done a damned fine job of it so far.

For forty-eight glorious hours, she'd put everything but him out of her mind. They'd talked and debated and plotted, between playing in the snow like children and feeding their insatiable appetites for each other. It was the world's best entirely unplanned vacation from her life. She felt energized, recharging with him in a way she hadn't since her whole crazy author career began.

But by the third day, the guilt had started niggling her. The sheriff's visit had reminded her that there was a life outside the four walls of the little cabin. She'd never been out of contact this long before. There were people she really ought to check in with in the real world, to let them know where she was and that she was okay. Plus they'd run out of condoms—even the two long strips that one of her friends had stuck in the side pocket of her bag as a party favor from Deanna's Thank God I'm Divorced party last summer. And wouldn't Jasmine be shouting a "You go girl!" for Ivy having pulled *that* off?

So they'd driven into Eden's Ridge to take care of necessary business. Arrangements had been made with Thompson's Garage to retrieve her Blazer from the side of the mountain. Not that anybody was under a delusion that it wasn't totaled, but they couldn't just leave it there. Willie Thompson, a grizzled old guy in overalls and a black trucker cap proclaiming "Good Guys Wear White," was totally going in a book someday. They'd done some shopping and finally ended up having lunch at the diner.

The call with her parents had gone fine. She'd downplayed the wreck and glossed over her current lodging situation. The preacher's daughter did not want to admit she was cozily and intimately shacked up with her rescuer. But she hadn't been able to force herself to call Marianne, even though she'd probably already booked a plane ticket to carry out her threat to hunt Ivy down if she didn't hear from her by—oh hell—yesterday.

"I could. But it would get to you eventually. Whether that's before or after she tracks you down is up for debate. So suck it up and get it over with, Blake."

Ivy winced. "Marianne's going to kill me."

"If she doesn't grant you an automatic extension for having been in a life-threatening wreck a few days ago, she's not human."

"It wasn't life-threatening. You were there."

His smile flashed white against his beard. "Yeah, but she doesn't know that. You're a writer. Control the image you portray. You were traumatized. Your laptop was killed in the accident. You're going to have to start over because the cloud backup didn't work."

She arched a brow. "It's a little disturbing how readily you have those excuses ready."

"I'm motivated by purely selfish reasons."

"Do those reasons involve getting me naked again as soon as we get home?" Ivy felt her teasing grin freeze. Home?

"They just might."

She barely heard his reply. Had she really just called the cabin home? What was up with that? Yes it was a cozy little love nest. But thinking of it as home was ridiculous. It was neither theirs nor home. And how would she, of all people, even know what that felt like anyway? But the sentiment was there nonetheless.

Or maybe it wasn't the cabin. Maybe it was Harrison himself. She felt more grounded and stable with him than she had in...

years. Maybe ever. Maybe there was some kind of hero worship thing going on—and there was definitely phenomenal sex—but there was more, too. He was slowly but surely opening up to her. As she'd relaxed and settled, so had he, though he still had a tendency to err on the side of turning the conversation back to her or the book rather than talking much about himself. They hadn't discussed anything beyond the now. The now was so very unexpected and wonderful, she was afraid to say anything to risk jinxing it.

But that hadn't stopped her from thinking about it. The idea of a relationship hadn't even been on her radar since grad school. She barely managed to keep up with her friends. And yet she was already wondering what she'd have to do to keep Harrison as part of her real life. Would he want that? Would the fantasy hold up under the harsh light of the everyday? She wasn't ready to find out just yet.

If Harrison noticed her gaffe, he made no indication. "Would it help if I offered to reward you for being a good girl and making that call?" His devilish grin made it clear what kind of reward he had in mind.

"Do I get to pick the reward?"

"Sure, why not?"

"Okay, then after I make the call, I get to ask you a question about you and you have to answer."

Some of his humor fled. "Why?"

"Because you're really good at deflecting. We've talked a lot about me the last few days. I want to know about you."

He shifted in his seat. "I'm out of practice with sharing anything about myself."

"One question, Harrison."

"Fine. With the qualifier that there's stuff I can't talk about because it's classified."

"Much as that intrigues me, that isn't the stuff I want to know." Ivy took a breath. "Okay. I'm doing this."

She punched in Marianne's number.

"Ivy,wherethehellhaveyoubeen? I'vebeentryingtoreachyoufordays!" Marianne's greeting spewed out without a single breath or pause, loud enough that Harrison obviously heard from across the table.

He arched a brow.

"I'm sorry I didn't call before now. I was in an accident last week."

"Oh my God, are you okay?"

"I'm not permanently damaged. I can't say the same for my Blazer. I went over the side of a mountain. It was...bad."

"Ivy!"

"Nothing's broken, but I've been pretty shaken up. I had to be treated for exposure and a minor head injury." She looked up at Harrison and saw his eyes darken at the memory.

"I'm so glad you're okay."

"Well, I may not be when you get through with me. My laptop died in the crash. And my backup to the cloud failed. The book's gone."

Marianne sucked in a breath. "Gone? Like...gone gone?"

"Yeah."

"How is that possible? Can't they pull your hard drive and get the data?"

"It was damaged, too." She was possibly going to a special writer's hell for this lie. "I've already started rewriting, but I'm going to need an extension."

"Wally's not going to be happy about this."

"It's not like I planned to drive off the side of a mountain."

"Of course not."

"I've never asked for an extension in the entire time we've worked together, Marianne. I need this."

"Okay. I'll talk to him. But Ivy, I don't know how much of an extension he can get you. They were counting on slotting you in for a summer release and you know how long the rest of the process takes. The only reason you've been able to get away with things this long is your first drafts tend to be so clean."

"I know. Just...do whatever you can, okay? I'm going head down and writing as fast as I can." A fresh flush of guilt crept over her. She hadn't done that. Not yet. She'd been enjoying a very sexy distraction.

"I'll call him now. If you can send me anything...anything at all. First chapter. First few chapters by tomorrow, it will give me more leverage."

"Tomorrow?" Ivy's stomach did a swoop. She had an outline now. One that she knew, deep down, would actually work. But *tomorrow?*

"I know you can do it. You're my rockstar."

Ivy blew out a breath. For just a moment, she considered telling more lies—anything to buy more time. But she'd done enough evading. "I'll do my best."

She said goodbye and hung up the phone, already feeling the pressure pressing down.

Harrison offered a rueful smile. "Playtime's over, huh?"

"Yeah." Knotting her hands she met his gaze. "I don't want it to be. But there's not a chance in hell I'll get this book written if I stay with you."

"Do you think you can write it now, away from me?"

She thought about the detailed outline she'd been weaving together for the last several days and didn't feel the trepidation and blankness that had gone alone with her previous attempts. "Yeah. This one's solid. Largely thanks to you."

He scrubbed a hand over his face. "Well, then I have a proposal."

"I'm listening."

"You came up here intending to take a room at the inn and write, right?"

"Yeah."

"So do that. Stick with the original plan. And for every, say, ten thousand words you knock out, you take a break to see me and get to ask another of your questions. By the end of the book, you'll have gotten in quite a few. Do you suppose that'd be sufficient motivation?"

He still wanted to see her. He wasn't ready for this to end either. Relief tempered the pressure building in her chest.

"Yeah, it would. But even with me writing my ass off, that's going to take some time."

Harrison leaned both elbows on the table. "That's fine. I'm not going anywhere."

To have him waiting for her on the other side of all this—and all the milestones between—was a greater gift than she'd expected to get. So she'd take it.

"Then I guess I'd better see if I can get a new reservation."

CHAPTER 11

"You wanna grab a beer?"

On the other end of the line, Porter hesitated. "It's not even five yet, man."

Harrison glanced at his watch, though he knew perfectly well what time it was. "It will be in about forty-five minutes. I haven't made it all the way to town yet." The town limit sign that flashed by the Jeep window made a liar out of him, but why mention it?

"Is everything okay?"

Sure it was. Except the cabin felt empty without Ivy.

Harrison had expected that the first night. They'd been constantly in each other's company, in each other's space, for the better part of a week. He'd known he'd miss having her in his bed. But he'd expected to re-acclimate to the solitude. That was, after all, his preferred natural habitat.

When he'd dropped her off at The Misfit Inn, they'd made a plan to meet up tonight for dinner. Since she had no car and there was no way to reach him at the cabin by phone, it was the only logical option. Two days was enough of a span for her to get a serious start on the book. After all the brainstorming about Annika and Michael, he felt jazzed to go back to his own work.

He didn't have the deadline she did, or anybody else depending on him, but he did have to decide what came next in his own books. He figured he'd follow her example and go head down until she surfaced again. That had been forty-six hours ago, and he'd still found himself looking up at every sound, expecting her to be there.

It was better than the alternative of having his ghosts come back with a vengeance, but he missed her, damn it. Like some lovesick teenager, he'd even been counting down the hours until it was time to leave for Eden's Ridge. He didn't miss women. Well, in all fairness, he hadn't been truly involved with one in years. But he missed Ivy, and he didn't know what to do with that. How could he miss someone who hadn't even been in his life before the last week? Disgusted with himself, he'd decided to head into town early. Anything would be better than being left to his own devices.

"Yeah, everything's fine. You up for meeting at the Tavern when you finish up at the job site?"

"Sure. See you there."

Good. Maybe a visit would help mitigate this itch he'd had.

Knowing he had time to kill, he parked at one end of Main Street and figured he'd walk a bit. The sidewalks had been cleared, but there were still patches of white in corners and cracks where the salt hadn't reached. In the little park, a parade of misshapen snowmen were in various stages of death throes, as they melted with rising temperatures. Soon they'd be nothing but a puddle of memories.

He wondered if the same could be said of his affair with Ivy. That was really what was at the heart of this restlessness. For all he hadn't been looking and hadn't expected to find something with her, he had. What if she'd come to her senses the past couple of days? What if he really had been nothing more to her than a distraction? What if the easy intimacy they'd shared was gone and this dinner he'd been so looking forward to was awkward?

And what if you get a damned grip on yourself and stop making problems where there are none?

But it was his nature and his training to consider the possible disasters and how to handle them.

So start with the problem directly in front of you. You missed her. Do something to show her that.

Spying a shop with a profusion of blooms in the display window, Harrison crossed the street. The interior of Moonbeams and Sweet Dreams smelled lush and sweet, the fragrant flowers scattered around the store perfuming the warm air. Music played quietly from hidden speakers—some kind of Celtic fiddles and drums. From the back, a dog barked, and a woman's low voice quietly shushed it. A few seconds later, she emerged from a doorway behind the counter. For a moment, he could only blink at the crown of baby roses woven into her auburn hair, and the long, flowy skirt and top. Had he walked through a portal back to Woodstock?

"Can I help you?"

He blinked. "I'm gonna go out on a limb here and say you're a florist?"

The woman beamed. "I am. I'm Misty Pennebaker. Do you need some flowers?"

Flowers. Yeah. He'd take Ivy flowers. They'd be a a nice gesture. His mom had always appreciated unexpected flowers.

"I do."

"What's the occasion?"

"A woman."

Misty's lips bowed up in delight. "The very best occasion. Tell me about her."

How was he supposed to reduce Ivy to a simple list of descriptors? "She's smart and funny and interesting. And gorgeous." All true, but not the heart of who she was. He was still learning that.

"A romantic interest, then. And what do you want to tell her?"

"Tell her?"

Misty slid onto a stool behind the counter, grabbing a pen and notepad. "Sure. Flowers are their own language. So what do you want to tell your lady?"

"She's not mine. Exactly. It's...complicated, I guess. We haven't defined it."

"But you want to. Define it, that is."

Yeah. He did. He wanted this to be...something. He didn't know how, didn't know exactly what, but he knew he couldn't just walk away from the connection they'd shared. So he nodded. "But I don't want to be pushy. Or needy. I just want something that says...I've been thinking of you. Something that will wow but not overwhelm." Might as well go all-in.

Misty was nodding. "I can do that. Are these for delivery?"

"I was hoping I could take them with me when I pick her up for dinner tonight."

"I can work with that."

And she did. Half an hour later, Harrison walked out with an explosion of bright blooms, almost none of which he could name. Misty had assured him they were perfect, but he wondered if it was too much. Maybe he should've gone with something simpler, like daisies or tulips.

"Aw, flowers. You shouldn't have."

Harrison jerked his attention up from the bouquet to find Porter grinning at him from the sidewalk. The back of his neck heated. So much for getting a chance to stash them in the Jeep before hitting Elvira's.

"I didn't think you'd be done yet."

"It sounded like you had something on your mind, so I wrapped a little early. I'm guessing it's not so much some*thing* as some*one*."

Harrison resisted the urge to tuck the flowers behind his back. "I was just..." Just what?

Porter crossed his arms, his smile widening as Harrison floundered for something to say.

"Fine, I've got a date later." Why did he feel so stupid saying that? He was sharing a meal with the woman he'd been sleeping with. What else did you call it?

"Uh huh. With the woman you rescued, I take it. The one you were hanging out with shirtless when Xander showed up."

"So?"

"He said you two looked awfully…cozy for a couple folks who didn't know each other before this snowstorm."

Had the two of them been gossiping like a couple of teenage girls? Harrison scowled. "If you're gonna bust my chops, you're buying."

"With pleasure, brother."

Porter didn't give him a chance to stow the bouquet before heading to the tavern. This early it wasn't crowded, so they had their pick of tables.

A waitress sashayed over as soon as they sat down. "What can I get you boys?"

Porter held up two fingers. "Two beers, Trish. That new lager on tap. Thanks."

"Comin' right up."

With nowhere else to put them, Harrison laid the flowers on the far side of their four-top. He felt horribly conspicuous, like he'd accidentally worn hunter's orange instead of camo to a covert op. The sensation only increased as Trish came back with their drinks.

"Oh, those are simply gorgeous! Who's the lucky lady?"

Did she honestly expect an answer to that? Her expectant stare suggested she did.

Evidently taking pity on him, Porter flashed a smile at the waitress. "This'll be all, Trish. Thanks."

As soon as she'd walked away, Harrison took a healthy swallow of beer. He hated being the center of attention.

"So, you've had an eventful week for a guy who planned to be a hermit."

"Guess so."

"From what I hear, Ivy's pretty lucky you came along. Xander said the wreck was bad."

Harrison thought of the terrain on the side of that mountain. "The whole thing could've gone FUBAR pretty easily. Another few feet in either direction and she wouldn't have survived the crash. As it was, she came out with minimal injuries."

"Obviously you couldn't get her to town that night because of the weather. But I find it very interesting that when a ride presented itself, she elected to stay with you. I find it even more interesting that you let her."

"Was I supposed to just kick her out? Say, 'Oh, glad you're okay. You're no longer my problem. Good luck and Godspeed?' I'm not that much of a dick."

Unperturbed, Porter just lifted a brow. "Did you want to say any of that?"

"Does it matter?"

"I think it does."

Harrison sipped more beer. "No, I didn't want to say any of that."

"You actually wanted her to stay."

"Yeah. I did. So what?"

"So, it's telling. You connected with this woman."

Uncomfortable with the truth of his observation, Harrison curled his lip in a smirk. "Is that what we're calling it these days?"

Porter didn't bite. "You don't buy flowers for a woman you're just hot for. You don't let her stay for days, interrupting your planned solitude. This woman is important to you."

She was. And that Porter so easily recognized it made Harrison realize he must be walking around with his heart on his sleeve. Which meant he was in this a helluva lot deeper than he meant to be.

"It looks good on you," Porter continued.

"What does?"

"Living. You've been going through the motions the last few years. It's good to see you really reaching for something."

Harrison stared at him. "You got all that out of some gossip from your sheriff buddy and some flowers?"

"I got all that from the look on your face when you talked about her."

"What look?"

"The look that says you found somebody who's worth staying in the now and looking to the future instead of hanging in the past."

"The alternative is that she looks at the opportunities she's presented with and actively chooses life, chooses to engage, chooses to feel."

IT REALLY WAS A CRYING shame not to take time to linger in the claw-foot bathtub, but Ivy was far too hyped up to simply sit, languishing in bubbles. The book was *cooking*. So much so that she'd set herself five alarms to make sure she was ready early for her dinner with Harrison, lest she get sucked in again and still be in her author's uniform of leggings, an ancient sweatshirt from her alma mater, and a messy bun, with no makeup when he arrived. Not that he hadn't seen her looking the worse for wear, but she wanted to wow him when he came to get her, in case he'd been rethinking the wisdom of their involvement.

Things between them had escalated so quickly because of the close-quarters circumstances. Gaining some distance had been necessary for work, but what if he'd changed his mind about her? What if she'd built up this whole fantasy about what they were or could be to each other and the guy who came to get her was... something else? What if the intimacy they'd shared had been an illusion? Those questions had been enough to scare the crap out of her, so she'd buried herself in the book, throwing Annika unavoidably into Michael's path. Better to force him to face facts than make herself crazy facing her own.

But now she'd stepped away from the book and all those insecurities had come roaring back to the forefront. How should she greet him? Probably grabbing him by the shirtfront and dragging him into her room wasn't the way to go, no matter how much she wanted to. A hug? A kiss on the cheek? Should she take the lead or wait to see what he did? Would she have to start all over earning his trust? Or would he be the same guy who'd blown her brain with a lingering kiss on the porch when he'd left two days ago?

Because she was perilously close to pacing the floor, Ivy sat back down at her laptop.

"If you're gonna make anybody nuts, do it to Michael."

She fell back into the story, deep enough that when the knock came on the door some time later, it took her a few moments to register where she was.

Harrison.

Her heart leapt with nerves and excitement. Shoving back from the desk, she rushed across the room in bare feet, pausing with her hand on the knob to try to get herself under control so she didn't look as over-eager as she felt. Sucking in a few calming breaths, she fixed a smile on her face and opened the door.

A massive bouquet of flowers blocked her view.

Flowers?

Lifting her gaze, she spotted Harrison behind them, ears faintly pink, looking hella uncomfortable.

The fixed smile melted into a genuine one. "You brought me flowers? Awww." Reaching out, she accepted them from his outstretched hand and buried her face in the sweet-smelling blooms.

All the nerves, all the angst and questions, seeped out of her. He'd brought her flowers. A man didn't bring flowers to a woman he didn't actually like or was planning to break things off with.

Flowers—especially flowers like these—took a little thought and planning. So he'd been thinking of her as she had him.

A little giddy with relief, she grinned up at him. "Come in."

After a moment's hesitation, he stepped into her room. Belatedly, she looked around, wondering what state she'd left the place in. Thankfully, she hadn't been deep in the book long enough for it to turn into a pig sty. There was no pile of dirty clothes in the floor and the bed was actually made, courtesy of the inn staff. Of course, that just had her thinking about tumbling him onto it and mussing that neat comforter.

"These are beautiful. I'll have to ask Pru for something to put them in."

Fidgeting a little, Harrison scrubbed a hand at the back of his neck. "I should've thought of that."

Wanting to put him at ease, she lifted to her toes and brushed a kiss to his cheek. "You thought of *me*, which I appreciate. Thank you."

His hand slid around her waist, his dark eyes intent on hers in a way that made her stomach jump. "I've thought of little else the last couple of days."

She sensed the admission was hard-won. Maybe he'd struggled as much as she had being apart. Setting the flowers aside so they wouldn't get crushed, Ivy flowed into him, feeling all the nerves settle as his arms came around her. His broad hand slid into her hair, angling her head for a kiss. Then his lips were on hers and every doubt, every question faded.

She hadn't romanticized this, hadn't imagined it. He still wanted her and lord, did she still want him. Needing to get closer, she slid her hands up and over his shoulders to lock behind his neck. Maybe she could revisit that dragging him to bed scenario.

"Hey Ivy, did you need—oh!"

Feeling her cheeks go nuclear, Ivy pulled back to glance toward the still open door, where Pru's teenaged daughter, Ari, stood.

The girl didn't even bother to hide her smile. "Sorry."

Ivy had to clear her throat to speak. "It's fine. Did I need what?"

"I saw him bring in the flowers, so I thought you might need a vase." She held up the one she carried.

"That's very thoughtful. Thanks, Ari."

The girl stepped into the room, far enough to set the vase on a table. "I'm just gonna leave this here and get out of your way." Hastily backing up, she grabbed the door and swung it closed behind her. "Have a good night!"

Chuckling, Ivy dropped her head to Harrison's chest. "Well, now I feel way too weird to do what I really want to do."

"What's that?"

She lifted her head. "Show you exactly how soft and cushy this bed is."

Heat flared in his eyes. "There's always later."

"I like later."

"What about the meantime? How's the book coming?"

She pulled away, snagging his hand and dragging him over to her new laptop. Triumphant, she pointed at the bottom of the screen. "Behold that word count!"

Harrison went brows up. "You've cranked out nearly *seventeen thousand words* in two days?"

"Damned skippy! My brain is gonna be completely useless goo when this book is done, but it's going to be done. That's the important part."

"That's fantastic."

"What's even more fantastic is that it's *good*. Some of the best work I've done. I mean, I think. I'm probably not exactly unbiased at this stage. But I'm loving the story. I'm loving the chance to peel back their layers and show them as so much more than what the reader saw before." Squeezing his hand in gratitude, she smiled up at him. "You saw it first. I couldn't have done this without you. You've helped me fall back in love with writing again."

And maybe more than a little bit with you.

The realization slid between her ribs like a knife, leaving her stunned and only a few steps ahead of panic. *Oh God.*

It was too much, too fast. She hadn't meant for this to happen. She couldn't be in love with him. Not really. It was just lust. Wasn't it?

"Do you need to take notes?"

Ivy blinked up at him. "What?"

"You've got that distracted look, like you've just had a major plot realization. Do you need to write it down before we leave for dinner?"

That he'd think of that, respect that, made her heart go gooey. Damn it. This wasn't just lust.

"No. No, I definitely won't forget this." Squeezing his hand, she stepped away to find her shoes, grateful for the opportunity to hide her face for a moment. "Let's go get some dinner."

CHAPTER 12

"So I believe we had a deal." Across the table, Ivy leaned back in her chair, a glass of wine in her hand. "A question for every ten thousand words. I've earned a question and three quarters."

Damn. Harrison had hoped she'd forget. Not that he wasn't willing to share with her, but he was a little afraid of what she'd ask. "You can't ask a partial question."

She wrinkled her nose in a little snit that bordered on adorable. "Fine. I'll bank those seven thousand words for next time. I still get one."

You made the deal. Bracing himself, he picked up his beer. "So you do. Ask away."

"This has been circling around in my head since you dropped me off." She ran a finger around the lip of her glass, angling her head to study him. "What is it you do for a living that you can stick around here waiting on me?"

Of all the things she could've asked, that wasn't what he'd expected. Relief and mild embarrassment had him settling back in his own chair, rubbing a palm on his thigh. "Oh, that. Well, as it happens I'm also a writer."

Ivy blinked. "What?"

The stupefied expression on her face made him wish he'd said something sooner.

"Why didn't you tell me before?"

Self-conscious, he shrugged. "I'm not in your league. You're all multi-*New York Times* best seller, and I'm self-published. I mean, I do well enough. I make a living. But I figured you get all kinds of requests and shit from other aspiring or newly published writers who want an introduction or an in to the big leagues. I didn't want you to think I was one of them."

She waved a hand. "Oh, that whole snobby traditional vs. self-published debate is so five years ago. The indies have more than proven themselves savvy businesspeople. To my mind, you have it harder. You have to be author *and* publisher. I can't imagine doing more than I'm already doing."

"I'm not, really. I hire out my editor and cover artist. And I wager I do a lot less social media and fan stuff than you just because I don't have that kind of fan base. I don't have the acclaim, and I'm totally fine with that because it also means I don't have the pressure. There's no agent breathing down my neck, and my editor works on my schedule, not somebody else's. It's not a bad gig."

"No, I don't guess so." She dropped her head back and sighed. "No wonder you were so insightful about the problems I've been having. You *get* it."

"Well enough."

When she straightened, her eyes held a gleam of interest. "So what do you write?"

Harrison hesitated.

"Oh, come on. You can't just tell me you're a writer and not expect me to want to talk shop. This all still falls under the category of the first question I asked. Do you write thrillers, too? You're awfully damned good at helping plot them."

He shook his head. "I write science fiction."

"What kind of sci fi? Like...*Dune* or *Aliens* or space opera or what?"

"It's kinda *Firefly* meets *Game of Thrones* meets *Star Wars*."

Her eyes brightened. "That sounds epic. Why scifi?"

It was a logical turn of the conversation. She'd told him why she wrote thrillers. But the whys of his fiction skated a little too close for comfort to the ghosts he'd been struggling to escape.

Ivy's expression softened as she reached out to lay a hand over his on the table. "It's fine. I've used up my question."

What kind of coward was he, making her earn the right to know him? He wanted more with her than the physical, and that meant sharing more of himself, even the less than sterling parts. It meant choosing connection instead of avoidance and deflection. He wouldn't tell her all of it. Couldn't. But he could give her the gist.

Turning his hand over to curve around hers, he swallowed. "You weren't wrong in your profile. I left the Army three years ago. It was...a rough transition." *Captain of Understatement.* But he couldn't bring himself to revisit those first six months out. "I'd enlisted when I was eighteen, worked my way through the ranks. It's all I'd really known in my adult life. Those men and women were my family. And I'd lost three of them because of a call I made."

Her fingers tightened around his but she said nothing, offered no false platitudes. And somehow that made it a little easier.

Harrison sipped at his beer to wet his parched throat. "I didn't handle it well. I kept replaying it over and over, trying to see what I'd missed, what I could have changed that would've altered the outcome." He'd relived it too, for about eighteen months. But those attacks had come fewer and farther between. The one he'd had at the cabin had been his first in more than a year. But even that hadn't been a full-blown flashback. Thank God.

"My therapist suggested I write about it. She meant journaling, but that was too...close. Too personal. I couldn't look directly at it without ending right back up in the same place. So I ended up creating this character and shifting the whole damned thing to another world. Pretty soon, I'd come up with at least a dozen different variations for what could've happened differently. And most of them involved tech that doesn't actually exist, intel I didn't have. One impossibility after another. Because the reality was that there wasn't anything I could've done differently. Because I'm not God."

Those silver-green eyes shone with empathy.

"Yeah, you were right about that, too." He grimaced. "Knowing it doesn't make it any easier to live with. It doesn't changed what happened. But writing about it like that...it let me be God in some small way. And I found myself taking the strongest scenario of the lot and following what happened to those men, if they'd lived."

Her thumb stroked the back of his hand, a soft, soothing rhythm. "Did it help?"

"Some. I was always into adventures and scifi as a kid, and it turned out I had an aptitude for writing it. Since it meant I could set my own hours and avoid people, it seemed like the ideal job." He sighed. "Or it did. You aren't the only one struggling with writer's block."

"That's why you came up here? Same as me?"

"Something like that." He thought of Ty and wondered how his buddy was holding up. But he wasn't ready to talk about the funeral or the ghosts it had stirred up.

"Well, you were a hell of a plot doctor for my book. Maybe I can return the favor. Where are you stuck?"

"I have to decide if I can keep going."

"With the current book?"

"With any of it. I'm three books deep and the war they're fighting isn't over. I'm not sure it'll ever be over." Because he didn't know if his own ever would be. "The fourth book is dragging because I don't know how it ends. I don't know if my hero can keep fighting it. I don't know if *I* can keep fighting it. So I've been considering that maybe he goes out in a blaze of glory and I wrap the series."

Catching the look of distress on her face he squeezed her hand. "That's not some kind of metaphor. I'm not considering suicide. I just think maybe the writing thing has run its course. It started out a way to figure out how my men could've lived, and ended up being a way to sort of let them live on. That part was good. But it hasn't exorcised those demons, and I'm not sure putting all my thoughts and memories of that shit on paper—even with lasers and spaceships—is a good thing. Keeps them...too close for comfort."

Ivy was quiet for a long moment. "Maybe the answer lies in not trying to rewrite the past but in writing a different future. I don't know your story or the context for your hero, but maybe in order for you to leave the war behind, your hero does, too."

Harrison frowned. "Just have him walk away? What the hell would that even look like?"

"I don't know. But it's the third option that doesn't involve staying in the fight or making the ultimate sacrifice. It gives you room to write more stories. If that's what you want to do."

The idea of it circled around the back of his brain as they finished their meal. Did he want to write more stories? If he wasn't writing about the horrors of war, he didn't know what stories he would tell. But as he helped Ivy on with her coat and offered his arm to escort her back out to the Jeep, he knew the only story he was positive he wanted to continue was theirs.

HARRISON STAYED quiet on the drive back to the inn.

Ivy worried he was too much in his head. Maybe her questions had pushed those things he'd been trying to forget to the forefront. Her heart twisted at his unexpected decision to open up to her, at the knowledge of what it had to have cost him. She understood his reticence. Who would want to talk about going through hell? And yet, clearly the experience was still with him. He'd been living with it, by turns circling around it and attacking it head-on. And none of that had quite helped him accept it. Maybe nothing would but time, but that didn't stop her from wanting to help.

Her gut said he shouldn't be alone tonight. She was the one who'd circled into that territory and brought it up. He'd said himself she was a good distraction. She could do that much for him, at least. Keep him in the now, with her. So when they got to the inn, she reached out to take his hand. "Come up."

For a moment, she thought he'd demur. Then his fingers closed around hers.

He followed her quietly up the stairs. They didn't run into Pru's family or any of the other guests. Ivy unlocked her room, letting them inside. A single lamp cast a gentle glow over the room. The flowers she'd arranged in the vase before they left for dinner made the air smell sweet. Laying her purse beside them on the desk, she locked the door and turned to Harrison.

His focus was very definitely on her now. She liked how he watched her, as if she were the center of everything. His true north. It was fanciful and romantic, but it made her feel beautiful and sexy and simply more than she was.

Moving into him, she laid hands on his chest, rising to her toes to brush a kiss over his lips. Just the barest whisper of a touch instead of the greedy gulps they'd shared before. She didn't want to rush. Her hands slid inside his coat, stroking up and over his shoulders to push it off. He tugged her closer by the front of her coat, his fingers making short work of the buttons and repeating her gesture, sliding his hands down her spine and pulling her against the length of him.

All that warmth and strength was intoxicating. So was the taste of him as he took the kiss deeper, dipping his tongue into her mouth. Ivy lost herself for seconds, minutes, as her tongue stroked against his. Then he was peeling down her dress and following it with his lips, trailing them over each newly exposed inch of skin.

She could never get tired of this.

Because she knew he was apt to take over and she wanted her fill of him before he did, she fought her way through the haze of lust to unbutton his shirt, stripping it off and sliding up his under-shirt so she could press a kiss to the smooth, warm skin of his chest, over the heart that beat thick and fast to match hers. His chest rumbled with a groan of pleasure and his hand slid into her hair, holding her there for a long moment.

Ivy lifted her gaze to his and felt her own pulse trip. There was the intensity she'd come to crave and lust as well. But beneath all that she saw an unexpected vulnerability. As if he were willingly dropping those shields, letting her in.

She reached up to frame his face, murmuring his name as she kissed him again, trying to say without words what she hardly dared admit to herself.

I love you.

It was so, so easy to lose herself in him. She could only hope he felt the same.

He stripped off her bra, following the strap with his mouth as he drew it away, then bending to take one nipple into his mouth. Her knees buckled, but he was there, lifting her up until her legs could wrap around his waist, fitting the bulge of his erection against her center. Needing more pressure, more friction, she shimmied against him. His hands dug into her ass with something close to a growl. Then they tumbled onto the bed and the weight of him was gone as he tore his mouth away to strip off her underwear.

She started to make a complaint, a demand, but then he pressed that mouth to her core and she couldn't do anything but gasp his name, burying her fingers in his hair as he drove her slowly, ruthlessly up. He battered her with waves of delicious sensation, bringing her closer and closer, until she was wrecked and aching and breathing his name like a prayer for deliverance. Only then did he push her over. She barely bit back a cry as the orgasm pulled her under like a riptide.

The bed dipped and creaked as he crawled into it, fully naked. But he didn't cover her, didn't settle himself between her thighs. Instead, he stretched out beside her, stroking a soft hand through her hair, down her arm, over the flare of her hip as she trembled with aftershocks.

"You're so beautiful."

When he looked at her like that, she felt it.

Rousing herself she rolled toward him, reaching out to touch and taste. He fell back, letting her explore the body she'd come to know so well in so short a time. She'd noted the scars before, the physical reminders of the life he'd led. She'd skipped over them, not wanting to draw undue attention. He hadn't told her about any of them. But she'd done enough research that she understood the kind of wounds that had caused each one. They'd all long healed, some better than others. But they represented deeper wounds, wounds she wanted to combat with tenderness. So this time she paused to press a slow, lingering kiss over each of them, tracing her fingers, then her lips over the puckered flesh high on one shoulder where a bullet had ripped through.

Harrison stiffened, and Ivy hesitated, eyes flying to his face. He let out a long, controlled breath, his dark eyes watching her, saying nothing as she slowly lowered her head to press a lingering kiss to the old wound. He relaxed degree by slow degree as she continued. The slash where a knife had glanced off his ribs. The knot in his thigh where he'd been caught by some kind of shrapnel. With endless patience and tenderness, she made love to his warrior's body, until he exhaled her name, reaching out for her. "Need you now."

Her heart squeezed. To be needed by this man, who was so capable, so in control.

He dragged her up his body, his hands curling around her hips in blatant possession as he urged her to straddle him. She kept her gaze on his as she rolled on a condom and lined up their bodies, then she reached out to cradle his face as she took him in. His eyes went to slits, but they stayed locked on hers as he thrust up to meet her. Her moan of satisfaction was long and low, a counterpoint to his reverent curse. Bracing herself against his chest, she rode him, keeping a slow, torturous pace, wanting to draw out the pleasure as long as possible. And when they both began to crest, she took his mouth, swallowing his groan of release with her own before collapsing in a boneless heap.

Harrison recovered first, carefully pulling out and going to take care of necessities before coming back to bed and dragging her against his chest in a spoon. She snuggled in, enjoying the feel of his hand stroking lazy patterns on her belly and the solid presence of him at her back.

She wanted this. This comfort, this warmth, this connection. For longer than the next week. Longer than the next month. It was easy to spin a fantasy where this was their new normal. Where she wrote and he wrote, and they lived a perfect and lovely creative life. And that was probably nuts. How could this—just this—feel so much like a foundation so fast?

But there it was. Being with him just felt...right.

She couldn't say any of that yet. It was too much, too fast. And they'd already been moving at warp speed. But she could ask for tonight.

"Will you stay?" she murmured.

He inhaled a slow breath and pressed a kiss to her shoulder. "No."

That had her eyes popping open, ripping her afterglow to tatters. "No?"

"You have work to do. If I stay, you'll be up half the night and in no shape to write tomorrow."

She rolled to face him. "But—"

"You know I'm right." The curve of his lips was smug and cocky, but there was something else there she couldn't read.

Maybe that was her imagination. The orgasms had fried her brain. He wasn't wrong. "Sometimes I hate it when you're practical."

"You'll thank me later."

She probably would, but that didn't change the fact that she'd miss him. Again. "When can I see you again?"

"If you got seventeen thousand words by not seeing me for two days, how much can you knock out if it's longer?"

Ivy scowled. "That is not the kind of carrot on a stick I was hoping for, Harrison."

He chuckled. "Maybe not. But I need to get some work done, too. I want to think about what you said, make some decisions about this book and my series. And I can't do that if I've got the temptation of seeing you sooner than the end of the week."

She was pouting. A full on lip-poking snit like she hadn't had since she was a kid. She knew it, but she couldn't seem to stop herself. "The end of the week?"

Harrison kissed her again and rolled away to begin dressing. She couldn't help but feel like it was a rejection. In the absence of his warmth, she pulled the covers over her breasts.

He tugged on his t-shirt. "Friday. Let's plan for Friday. And get as much as we both can done, with the expectation of taking more than an evening's break. We'll spend the weekend together."

The prospect of more time together was pretty appealing. And if she really dove deep, maybe, *maybe* she could be nearly finished. Or close enough she could send stuff to Marianne and buy a reprieve to focus on him again.

"Well, if that's the best deal I'm gonna get, I suppose I'll have to take it. But early Friday. Like, mid-afternoon."

"Sounds like a plan."

She started to reach for her own clothes. "I'll walk you down."

Harrison put a hand on her shoulder, pressing her back to the bed. "No, I can see myself out. And I'd rather have the image of you naked and sated in my head to keep me warm on the way home."

She arched a brow. "Is that the look on my face right now?"

The easy rumble of his laugh put her back at ease. "I'd say you're somewhere between sated and pissed."

"Sounds about right."

"Hang on to that for Friday. You can have your wicked way with me as many times as you want."

Scooping a hand through her tangled hair, she fixed him with a Look. "I'm holding you to that."

He grinned. "I'm counting on it." With another fast, hot kiss, he was gone.

Ivy fell back on the bed, one arm across her eyes. This wasn't how she'd wanted the night to end, damn it. But he was probably right about the productivity. So she'd better just make the most of it and finish the damned book.

CHAPTER 13

*W*alking away from Ivy the other night had taken all Harrison's self control. It had been harder than leaving her at the inn the first time, harder to go back to the echoing emptiness of the cabin, knowing he wasn't likely to find what he'd originally come for. But it had still been the right thing for both of them in the moment. She needed to work. He needed to get his head on straight. Because he was having all kinds of way-too-serious, way-too-fast thoughts, and if he'd stayed, he wouldn't have been able to resist sharing them and scaring her the fuck away.

The obvious answer had been to remove himself from temptation. And he'd meant what he'd told her. He needed to think about what she'd said over dinner.

"Maybe the answer lies in not trying to rewrite the past but in writing a different future. Maybe in order for you to leave the war behind, your hero does, too."

Cooper Royce believed in the mission. Even when the mission was hopeless. He knew there was no end to the war, not in his lifetime. But still he fought because he believed it was the right thing to do. He had to have purpose because...Harrison had to have purpose. The point of the books had been to explore those million-and-one what-if scenarios and to let his men live on in some small way. He'd done that. So what purpose was left? For him? For Coop?

Harrison didn't see himself just writing for the sake of writing. He enjoyed it. But he needed a stronger *raison d'être* to keep exploring the hell he'd been through. Then again, that was Ivy's point. That maybe he—and Coop—needed to explore new frontiers. What would those be? Coop had far too strong a moral compass to walk away without a good reason. But he, like Harrison, had been feeling the strain of that endless, slogging fight, without making a difference.

You made a difference, at least for a few people.

He'd saved the dozen or so fan emails he'd received from struggling servicemen. Guys who'd left the military and struggled to adapt to civilian life. They'd all taken comfort in seeing their difficulties normalized, in reading his stories and recognizing themselves. Harrison didn't think he deserved their praise. He'd written the books for himself. For his men. He hadn't expected to touch anyone else.

The first one had made him weep. A former Marine, who'd lost both legs to a roadside bomb in the Middle East, had been on the verge of suicide when he'd fallen into the world of the Aegis Quadrant. He'd connected with Coop and seen something that made him willing to keep going, keep fighting to live another day. That email had been the thing that kept Harrison from going down the same path. There'd been others, each one a surprise, touching him at a soul-deep level. They'd somehow found the strength to keep going because Coop had. Because his indomitable spirit wouldn't allow him to do anything else. Because, at the end of the day, no matter how much he'd lost, somehow, he still managed to hold on to the rarest commodity in the galaxy—hope.

But Harrison didn't know how to keep selling that. Because,

truth be told, he'd been losing it himself, fighting this battle with his demons. If there was nothing to life but that, what was the point in staying the course? How could he not feel like a fraud putting that message out there? He hadn't been doing more than surviving. And he hadn't even realized it until Ivy.

She'd woken him up, kickstarted the lump in his chest that had died three years ago. She made him want to write a different future for himself, one that was a real life, not the shadow he'd been living. One that included her.

The knock on the door had Harrison shooting to his feet, his heart leaping in his chest like a puppy with a brand new ball.

Ivy.

He'd made it halfway across the cabin before he forced himself to slow the fuck down. She didn't have a car, so it probably wasn't her. Unless she'd had somebody take her to get a new one so she could surprise him? Fueled by that idea, he crossed the last few feet to the door, fighting the mile-wide smile that wanted to take over his face.

The sight of Porter on the porch drained away his excitement. The reaction wasn't fair to his friend, but Harrison wasn't feeling particularly rational just now. He stepped back automatically. "I really hope you brought beer."

"No."

The single, terse word had Harrison shaking off thoughts of a surprise booty call and zeroing in on Porter as he stepped inside, moving fast. His jaw was set, his eyes grave.

Harrison tensed, waiting for the blow. "What happened?"

"Ty went to see Garrett Reeves' widow."

"Shit." Harrison scooped a hand through his hair thinking about his own personal missions of visiting the families of the men who'd died under his command. They'd been worse than anything he'd seen in combat. "How bad is he?"

"Bad. Sebastian tracked him down, scraped him off a bar stool, and took him back home, but he could use some backup. Some of us who've been where he is."

And now he understood why Porter had come. "Are we talking intervention or suicide watch?"

"Both."

In all likelihood, this would involve peeling back the scab he'd worked so hard to build and exposing everything he'd been trying to get past. Reliving the trauma in a way even writing about it hadn't forced him to do. Harrison didn't relish any of it. But his brother-in-arms needed him. Nothing else mattered.

"I'll pack my things."

~

SOMEWHERE DURING THE last fifteen thousand words, Ivy's eyelids got replaced by sandpaper. She didn't give a damn. The book was finished. Or at least the first draft of it. There'd be revisions and line edits and galleys to proof before it ever made it to stores. And that was only if her editor actually went for it. But she had a finished book with a beginning, middle, and end. One she was actually pretty freaking proud of.

She should really email it directly to Marianne so she'd call off the hit man she'd probably hired by now. It was what Ivy had promised. And, really, she hadn't slept properly in days and had consumed well past the legal limit of coffee. She needed someone's balanced opinion to tell her if this book was really as good as she thought or if she was just flat crazy. But it wasn't her agent's opinion she craved. All she could think about was showing it to Harrison. This book had only been born because of him. She was dying to know what he thought of it. And, book aside, she just wanted to see him. She wanted that weekend of one-on-one time he'd promised as her reward.

Loading the book on a flash drive, Ivy snatched up her coat and headed for the stairs.

"Hey, Ivy."

She whipped around and saw Pru's daughter coming out of one of the rooms, a load of towels in her arms. "Hey, Ari."

"Where are you off to in such a hurry?"

"To see Harrison."

"Dressed like that?" The sincere shock in the girl's voice had Ivy pausing to look down.

She wore flannel pajama pants, a Tennessee Titans t-shirt with a coffee stain down the front, and bedroom slippers. It occurred to her she didn't remember the last time she'd showered. "What day is it?"

Ari shook her head. "Oh honey." Wrapping an arm around Ivy's shoulders, the girl steered her back toward her room. "It's Friday."

"Friday? Oh, then he's coming here." She checked her watch. "Ohmigod. He's due in like twenty minutes."

"C'mon. In the shower. I'm bringing you some of our creams from the spa. It'll help with those bags under your eyes."

Recognizing her own judgment was compromised, Ivy let herself be herded. Back in her room, Ari whistled. "Wow."

Ivy hadn't actually noticed the mess before now. The bed was a snarl of covers. Dirty clothes trailed over half the furniture. A couple of trays loaded with more than a dozen empty coffee cups were lined up in the floor along one wall. Only the space around her laptop was anything resembling tidy.

Embarrassment began to set in. "I'm really sorry about this. I'm not normally this much of a slob, but the book was going so well, and I just didn't notice. I'm done now, so I can pick up—"

"You finished the book?"

"The first draft anyway."

"That's *awesome!*" Ari gave her a celebratory squeeze. "Now, go get in the shower. I'll deal with things out here. And if he gets here before you're ready, we'll keep him busy." Without waiting for an answer, she shoved Ivy into the bathroom and shut the door behind her.

Because it was easier than arguing, and because the euphoria associated with *The End* had faded enough for her to register that she looked more like she'd slept in a barn for a week than in a nice, cozy inn, Ivy stripped and climbed into the shower. As soon as the hot spray hit her knotted muscles, she groaned, suddenly aware of every ache she'd blocked out during the long hours of sitting. Bracing her hands against the shower wall, she dropped her head and let the water beat at her back. Which just had her thinking about the shower at the cabin and all the deliciously wicked things they'd done in it.

But it wasn't the sex she'd missed—although that was amazing and she didn't want to think about going back to battery-assisted orgasms—it was him. He fascinated her. Behind that tough, taciturn attitude was a man who took care, did the right thing with little thought to himself. As independent as she'd always been, Ivy had never imagined she could find that so appealing. But he made her feel rooted and cherished and generally amazing. And she wanted more. She wanted this to go on past the right now. Was he ready to hear that? Could he look past the right now and into the future? She was ready to find out.

By the time she'd soaped, shaved, shampooed, and otherwise made herself presentable, Ari—and possibly a team of house elves —had worked miracles on her room. The bed was made with fresh linens, the trays had been whisked away, and the laundry was piled in a corner. She'd even unearthed clean clothes from Ivy's suitcase and laid them out on the chair. A little jar of face cream sat on the bedside table with a note propped on the side: *Use me.*

Ivy dabbed some on and dressed. Then, because sanity had returned, she emailed the draft to Marianne before walking out the door again. Ari was waiting in the hall.

Ivy stopped and held out her arms. "Am I presentable now?"

The girl grinned. "Much better. Go knock his socks off."

On impulse, Ivy hugged her. "Thanks, kid. Is he downstairs?"

Ari shook her head. "Maybe he's late?"

It was a half hour past when they'd agreed. He'd been early last time. But she shrugged off the vague worry and headed down to the guest lounge to hang out for a bit. When he hadn't arrived by the end of tea time, Ivy started to get worried. She wanted to call, but of course, with the communication issue, they hadn't even bothered swapping numbers. Because they were idiots.

Pru, clearing up the glasses from the other guests, shot her a sympathetic smile. "Why don't you borrow my car and go out to check on him?"

"You really don't mind?"

"Not at all. And if you cross paths, we'll set him straight."

On the drive out of town, Ivy managed to convince herself that he'd found a groove with his own book and lost track of time. She hadn't even known for sure what day it was until Ari told her. With every mile her anticipation grew, the book high melding with her excitement over seeing him again and a little bit of dread over that serious discussion she wanted to have. The temptation to sing the whole way was strong, but she needed to figure out what to say. She allowed herself one motivating anthem of Madonna's "Crazy For You" before focusing on the issue at hand.

"Harrison, the last two weeks have been amazing. You're pretty damned amazing, and I want to see you again. No strings. I know neither of us came here looking for this. I just...don't want you to slip out of my life because we didn't swap contact information." Her fingers drummed the steering wheel. "That's not threatening, is it? He gets to set the pace. I just want his freaking phone number and email address."

He wouldn't say no. Harrison Wilkes had made it clear he was into her.

Ivy was singing again by the time she made it to the cabin.

"Don't Stop Believin'" again. And that was a nice bit of circularity since it had sort of brought her to him in the first place.

But as she pulled into the drive, it wasn't Harrison's Jeep parked out front. An older model Explorer had the back hatch open. A woman came out of the cabin, juggling a caddy full of cleaners and nudging a vacuum cleaner.

"Can I help you?"

Ivy shoved away the confusion and went for a smile. "I'm sorry. I was looking for Harrison Wilkes. He's staying here. We were supposed to meet in town for dinner tonight, but I think we maybe got our wires crossed. Do you know what time he left?"

The woman hefted the vacuum down the steps. "No guests here now. The last one checked out."

"Checked out?"

She nodded.

This made no sense. They had plans.

"Was there a note of any kind?"

"Not that I saw, but if you want to step in and look around while I finish loading up, you're more than welcome to."

Ivy climbed the steps, a leaden cloak of dread replacing her elation. The interior was pristine. No crackling blaze in the fireplace. No books scattered on the coffeetable. There was nothing set out on the counters. It was an empty cabin, waiting for its next guest.

Maybe he'd gotten tired of being so cut off and wanted to come into town to stay? Ivy headed back outside. "Do you happen to know when the last guest checked out?"

"Couple days ago. I got the order to come out and clean yesterday, but I couldn't make it until today on account of my son had a doctor's appointment."

Two days ago. He'd checked out two days ago. He'd left no note, no forwarding address, hadn't been by the inn to see her. He was just gone, without a trace.

Harrison Wilkes, the man she'd fancied herself in love with, whom she'd wanted to talk to about pursuing a real relationship, had ghosted her.

~

SHIT. Shit Shit. I forgot to talk to Ivy. Why the fuck didn't I get her number so I could call or at least send a freaking text?

Not that he could send a text since his phone had been sent sailing into the lake when Ty took exception to their intervention. He hadn't dared leave his friend alone to get it replaced. It had been a harrowing few days, with little sleep and a lot of worry. He'd just lost track of time. He'd meant to call the inn on his way out of town to leave a message for Ivy, but the cell service was shit, and once he'd gotten to Georgia, things had gone so sideways with Ty, he couldn't think of anything else. But he'd never imagined he'd forget to call until hours after he was meant to pick her up.

Swiping Ty's phone off the nightstand, he found Porter in the contacts. He answered on one ring.

"Ty?"

Glancing at the bed, Harrison stepped out into the hall. "It's me."

"Why are you on Ty's phone?"

"There was an incident with mine. It's out of commission. Listen, I fucked up and forgot to let Ivy know I wasn't going to be back, and I missed picking her up this afternoon. I need you to get a message to her that I had an emergency, and I'll get in touch with her as soon as I can."

"Sure thing. How soon do you suppose that'll be?"

"Not sure. Ty's been down since yesterday. We'll see if he decides to rejoin the land of the living when he wakes up and go from there."

"Keep me posted."

The lump on the bed made a noise like a wounded buffalo.

"Sounds like he's waking up. Thanks, brother." Harrison hung up and went back into the bedroom. "You alive?"

Ty rolled onto his back and draped an arm over his eyes. "Debatable."

"You wanna be?"

He went still, the unsteady rise and fall of his chest the only thing indicating he was still awake. "Pretty sure Garrett would come back and haunt my ass if I said anything but yes."

After the last few days, that was progress.

"There's Gatorade and aspirin on the side table there."

Sucking in a breath, Ty shoved himself upright and winced. "Do I have anything to apologize for?"

"You mean before or after you got blackout drunk and tried to take a header into the lake?"

"Shit. How far did I get?"

"Not far." They'd made sure of that. Harrison wondered if he'd remember any of the last three days.

Ty tossed back a few pills with his Gatorade and wiggled his jaw. "Did I get into a fight?"

"Not exactly. I had to cold cock you to get your service weapon away from you."

He slowly lowered the bottle. "Did I try to use it?"

"Not on us." Harrison wouldn't soon forget the image of his friend with a gun barrel pressed to his temple.

Ty closed his bloodshot eyes. His voice, when he spoke again, was choked. "It should've been me."

"What should've?"

"I was the one who was supposed to be sitting shotgun that day. It should've been my leg blasted off. Me who died in that chopper. It was my fault."

Because he knew too well the guilt, Harrison kept his tone brusque. "Bullshit."

"But—"

"Did you plant that land mine? Did you tip off insurgents about the route? Did you pull that trigger against your own men?"

"Of course not."

"You did your fucking job. You defended your position and did everything you could."

"I couldn't save him." Ty dropped his head, his shoulders shaking.

Harrison reached out and grasped his hand, relieved when Ty held on instead of pulling away. "Sometimes you can't. It's part of war."

"I can't go back. I can't do another tour with that in my head, on my heart. I can't have anybody else's life in my hands like that."

"No shame in that. I couldn't go back either." Harrison sucked in a breath, bracing himself. This was what he'd come for, why Porter had dragged him here. Because he'd walked through this fire and come out the other side.

"I lost three of my men." Harrison swallowed past the razor-blades in his throat, wishing he didn't have to voice this again. "It was dead of winter in Afghanistan. Bitter cold. We came up on this woman, bleeding. She was hysterical, didn't speak a word of English, and all we could really get out of her is 'child,' and she kept pointing over the side. There was a car that had slid off the road. It was barely hanging on the side of that mountain. Driver's side door was open, and we could just see a carseat in the back. So we mobilized for a rescue."

Even now, after going over the setup a thousand times in his head, Harrison couldn't see the tell, couldn't find the clue that would've had him making any other decision.

"I'd gone back to the Hummer to radio our position and let command know we were gonna be a bit late, when the first shot rang out. My guys were over the side, all roped in. Fucking sitting ducks for the sniper hidden across the gorge. All three of them were dead in seconds, and I barely made it out. You wanna talk about guilt? About failure? I'm the one that made the call. I'm the one that put them on that mountainside. I'm the one who went to each of their families to tell them how I didn't smell an ambush."

More than anything else, those visits had nearly killed him. So he understood exactly why Ty's trip to see Bethany Reeves had sent him off the rails. If not for others doing for him exactly what he was doing now, he might've come to a different end. "I wish I could say it gets easier. It doesn't. It's a pain you have to learn to live with."

"How?"

Harrison thought of what he'd been doing. Of how he kept writing different versions of what happened, trying to exorcise it, trying to make everything come out different. It hadn't helped. Not really. Because what had happened was irrevocably a part of him. So much so that a woman who'd been a total stranger had seen it, in his eyes, in the lines of his face, down to the marks on his soul. She'd looked at him and seen hero material.

He didn't feel like a hero, but Ivy made him want to try. There was no going back to that mountain road and changing what happened. He'd been telling his stories through his books, but he'd been telling them for himself. He thought of the emails and wondered if that was the answer. Instead of story as therapy for him, story as service for them. He found himself wanting to do more. Wanting to tell stories for guys like Ty. Those guys coming home, who needed to see the same shit happening to someone else, somebody they could relate to. Somebody who could hear, "It wasn't your fault. There was nothing you could have done," and then realize that was true.

He needed to show them his truth. Which meant he had to accept it himself.

"You have to accept the fact that awful shit happens with no rhyme or reason, and you weren't to blame for those who died when you lived."

"I don't have the first clue how to do that."

"Neither did I. It's not an easy thing to let go of. But on the bad days, the days it feels like that can't be true, I remember what the wife of one of my men told me when I went to see her. She said if we hadn't stopped to try to help, if we hadn't immediately tried to save the child we thought was in danger, then her husband wouldn't have been the man she fell love with. We had no way of knowing it was a set up, so we did the right thing based on the information we had. Period."

"That helps?"

"Sometimes. In the end, you have to find a new mission."

This was his.

Even as Harrison thought it, ideas bombarded his brain.

Maybe there were guys out there who needed to see Coop do more than just keep going. Just like Harrison, he'd been surviving, not living. If Harrison had taken nothing else away from his time with Ivy, it was that. So maybe his readers needed to see Coop walk away, to choose life instead of death, instead of duty, to give themselves permission to do the same.

But what would that look like? How did people live far from the front, where death was less of a certainty? People whose every day wasn't shaped by the movements of troops or the acquisition of critical intelligence? They'd lead far simpler lives, where their biggest concerns were having basic needs met. And maybe, without the bitter mistress of duty, there'd be time for a woman.

What would it take to turn Coop's head? What sort of woman could make him see that there was more to life in the Quadrant than war and encourage him to embrace it? A sharp-eyed, whip-smart beauty with silky brown hair and eyes like winter forests, perhaps.

Of course it came back to Ivy. It seemed almost all his thoughts lately came back to her.

She'd have a field day profiling Coop. The idea of it made him smile.

Maybe he'd ask her when she was done with her own book and had a chance to actually maybe read his stuff. That was a terrifying thought. She was *good*. Terrifyingly so. He was...well, far better than adequate, but he'd have been lying if it didn't admit he was a little professionally intimidated by her. Or maybe it was less fear of how she'd like his writing and more about what reading it would reveal about him.

Maybe they could discuss the whole thing over dinner. After he explained his disappearing act.

"What kind of mission?" Ty's words interrupted his train of thought. "I've been in the Army since I was eighteen. I don't know anything else."

Harrison dragged his focus back to the conversation. He wouldn't be able to shake loose to drive back to Eden's Ridge for a while yet, but as soon as he got a minute, he'd try to get a message to her. "Why'd you go into the military in the first place?"

"I was a skinny ass kid. Bullied growing up. I wanted to become somebody who was in a position to protect others."

In Harrison's head, Coop traded in his proton rifle for a futuristic six-shooter and a badge.

"Have you ever considered a career in law enforcement?"

CHAPTER 14

*I*vy spent the trip back to the inn in a state of disbelief, trying to generate some alternative explanation where Harrison hadn't just walked away from her without a word. But all she could remember was the distance he put between them the last night they were together. He'd declined to stay, citing her need to work. And then he'd made it even longer until she'd see him again. Had he planned to leave even then?

No. She couldn't have been so wrong. Could she? There had to be some explanation. Right? Somehow, some way, there was an alternate reason for the fact he wasn't there. But good as her imagination was, she couldn't find a rational way to dismiss the fact that he'd checked out. He'd checked out. Himself. So it wasn't like he'd been in an accident and couldn't call. He'd left, like the proverbial thief in the night, and hadn't even had the decency to write a note or leave a message at the inn or even send up a freaking smoke signal to say, "Hey, it's been great, but I'm out. Sorry."

Apparently, she wasn't worth that courtesy.

"That son of a bitch." Her snarl of anger came out more like a wail. As the road began to blur, she realized she was crying. Damn it.

Had this whole affair been a lie? A way to get some tail before he went on to wherever he next had to go? Had he laughed at how easy a mark she was? The lonely writer who was so desperate for human connection, she'd throw herself at a veritable stranger. She'd been honest with him, vulnerable with him. And this was how he repaid her? Was he even a writer? There'd been no books listed under Harrison Wilkes when she'd searched online. Was anything he'd told her real?

She took a corner wrong and jolted as the two right wheels bumped up over the curb, eyes burning so badly, she could hardly see.

Somehow, she made it back to the inn without wrecking the borrowed car.

Pru looked up, startled, as she came through the door. "What—"

But Ivy just passed her the keys and went upstairs. As soon as she saw that big, comfy bed, she knew she couldn't stay here. Not here in this room and not here in this town, where everything would make her think of him. So she packed her bags, hauled them downstairs, and went to seek out her hostess.

Pru was in the office with Ari. The pair of them were practically bristling with questions, but neither said a word.

Ivy swallowed and forced the words out of a throat that felt like broken glass. "Is there any possible way someone could drive me to Johnson City to pick up a rental?" She should have done it earlier in the week, but she hadn't thought she'd need transportation just yet. She should have known better. Hadn't her life taught her to always have an escape plan?

"Flynn can drive you. But Ivy are you sure?" Pru looked like she wanted to say something else, but stopped herself.

"I'm sure." Maybe she owed them some kind of an explanation, but she just couldn't. She only wanted to be gone from here as fast as possible. Let them take in her tear-stained face and draw what conclusions they would. They'd be close enough to whatever constituted the truth.

Flynn, bless him, didn't ask. And once she'd secured the rental, he quietly squeezed her hand. "Be careful."

Unable to speak, she just nodded and squeezed back.

On the four-and-a-half hour drive back to Nashville, she cycled between crying and fury—at him for leading her on, at herself for not seeing what was happening. She'd always prided herself on being such a good judge of character. Failing so spectacularly was an insult to her pride as much as his actions were an insult to her heart. Both made her feel stupid.

She wanted the comfort of home, where she could lick her wounds in private. But when she pulled into her garage going on eleven-thirty that night, she didn't feel any relief. The little house she'd proudly bought with royalties from her first book just felt empty. Unable to face that, she fell face-first into bed and went straight to sleep, barely remembering to take off her shoes.

That night, her dreams were full of Harrison—or rather, his back, as she kept arriving places, only to find him walking away. She woke with gritty, puffy eyes and wet cheeks sometime around eight. Her body ached like the flu. The idea of facing the unpacking and the laundry and the grocery shopping and all the things that went along with coming home from a long stint away was too much. She dragged the comforter she'd cocooned herself in during the night over her head and vowed to go back to sleep. But a sound from somewhere in the house had her eyes popping open.

Someone's in the house.

She quietly untangled herself from the blankets and grabbed her phone from the nightstand to call 911. Dead. She hadn't plugged it in to charge last night. Tossing the phone, she looked around for some kind of weapon. Her foot kicked over a pair of her tall boots and she bit back a curse, as pain radiated up from her stubbed toe. Bending down, she snatched up one of the empty wine bottles she used as boot forms and clutched it like a club. Her heart leapt in a frantic tattoo as she edged open the door and eased down the hall toward the living room, where someone was moving around. She had a moment to remember Harrison leaping to protect her when she'd screamed in the cabin kitchen and wished he was here now to do the same, because the bottle in her hands felt insubstantial and pitiful as a weapon.

Holding her breath, she peered around the doorframe to look into the living room. The woman had her back to the hallway and seemed to be doing something by the windows. Not seeing a gun, Ivy stepped into the room and flipped on a light.

The blonde shrieked and whirled, dropping the thing in her hand with a wet thunk.

Ivy lowered her makeshift weapon. "Deanna? What the hell are you doing here?"

Pressing a hand to hear chest, a wide-eyed Deanna gasped, "You asked me to water your plants while you were away. Crap on a cracker, Ivy, you scared me to death. When did you get home?"

"Last night."

Deanna looked down at her feet to the watering can spilling its contents all over the carpet. "Oh hell."

"I'll get towels."

Together they mopped up the mess.

"I'm gonna guess by the fact that you look like you've been hit by a truck, the book is either going really well or really badly."

Ivy jerked a shoulder. "The draft is turned in."

"That's great!"

"Wonderful." She knew she sounded like she'd just been told she needed a root canal. Without anesthesia.

Hands on hips, Deanna frowned. "Aren't you happy to be home?"

At the word "home," Ivy burst into tears. Because it didn't feel like home. It had before she went to Eden's Ridge because she simply hadn't known the difference. All these years moving around, she'd chased an idealized picture of what home really meant. She'd thought she'd built that for herself here, pouring in time and energy into painting walls and picking out furniture and hanging up art. And she loved her house. But that's all it was. A house. Because now she knew what she'd been missing all these years. And she wouldn't get that back because home wasn't the cabin or Eden's Ridge. It was him. Or who she'd thought he was.

Deanna pulled her into a hug. "Oh honey, tell me who he is and we'll plot his demise."

Ivy swiped at her face. "How do you know it's a guy?"

"You were with me through my divorce. I know what crying over a man looks like. Come on. I'll make you coffee."

They retreated to the kitchen and over two cups of coffee, Ivy spilled the whole thing out.

"I just...I don't know how I could have gotten things so wrong. I thought we were on the same page. Why would he make specific plans to meet me, to spend another weekend with me, if he was planning to leave all along?"

"Because men are cowards at heart," Deanna declared. "They'll do anything to avoid confrontation. And if you do catch them in a lie, they'll turn it around and blame it all on you, saying you made them do it."

Ivy wasn't entirely sure she agreed with that assessment. But the avoidance of confrontation? Yeah maybe that was a thing here. Things between them had been intense. Maybe too intense for him, in the end. There'd been a new vulnerability in him that last night. She knew she hadn't imagined that. So maybe this wasn't about using her and leaving her high and dry. Maybe this was about him not being able to handle things and running away.

And maybe you're projecting because that's what you do.

From back in the bedroom, her phone began to ring. Ivy didn't realize she'd expected it to be Harrison with some kind of explanation until she saw Marianne's name on the display and felt herself deflate.

"Hello?"

"Ivy, thank God. I was getting ready to send out the National Guard. I got your manuscript"

Cringing, Ivy waited. "Yeah?"

"This isn't what we discussed with Wally."

Whatever lingering pleasure she'd had over finishing the book wilted. This was it. Her career was done. "No, it's not. I couldn't make it work. I've been trying for the last eight months. It just wouldn't gel."

"This was so worth the wait. It's *good*, Ivy. Rough around the edges, but maybe the best thing you've ever done. Adding in that romantic thread is going to expand your readership. Where did that even come from? You've never done romance before."

I'm not doing it now.

"It was just an idea I wanted to play with. I don't know where it's going yet for the series, but there's a series there. If you think Wally will go for it."

"Go for it. Girl, he's already having kittens. He wants to get started on revisions as soon as possible."

You're not going to get what you don't ask for.

"Marianne, I need a break. I'll polish the book, but I need *time*. I'm burned out—dangerously so—and I have got to have more padding in the schedule. I can't sustain the pace we've had going."

"I figured you'd hit that point eventually. And that's fine. I'm pretty sure I can negotiate for more time. But Wally's going to want something in return." Her tone had turned speculative.

Ivy braced herself. "What did you have in mind?"

～

"GONE? What do you mean she's gone?"

"As in she went home last night." Porter's patient voice did nothing to calm the panic kicking against Harrison's ribs. "How? She doesn't have a car."

"Apparently Pru's husband gave her a ride to Johnson City to pick up a rental."

"Fuuuuuck." Harrison pressed his fist to his temple, wishing it would help alleviate the sudden icepick headache that had taken up residence behind his left eye. "And there's no message? Nothing for me?"

Porter's pause spoke volumes. "Well, no. She was pretty upset. It took me a little bit to explain to Pru what happened and actually get her contact information."

Harrison sat up, feeling hope kindle in his chest. "You got her contact info. Thank Christ."

"Well, sort of."

"Sort of? What the hell does that mean?"

"Well, all they had was her billing address. Which is a P.O. Box."

"A P.O. Box. How, exactly, is that helpful?"

"Because she lives in Nashville."

Nashville. Impossibly, miraculously, the woman of his dreams actually lived in the same town he did. Maybe there was a God.

"Okay. Okay, I can work with that. Thanks, man."

He had to track Ivy down. Of course she was upset. He hadn't shown. Hadn't contacted her. From her perspective, he'd just bailed. There was no telling what brand of asshole she imagined him to be. God, he hoped it hadn't derailed the book for her.

Ty stumbled into the kitchen. "What's going on?"

"Where's your computer?"

"What?"

Harrison slid off the barstool. "I need your computer."

Ty ducked into the fridge and came up with a bottle of water. "First my phone, now my computer. What do I look like? A Best Buy?"

"Brother, I love you, but if you don't show me where your

computer is right now so that I can start fixing the mess I'm in with the woman I left high and dry to be here, I'm going to be forced to kick your ass. And I'm not the one who smells like sweaty bourbon."

Ty lowered the bottle slowly. "You've got a woman?"

"I had a woman," Harrison corrected. "Who I was supposed to pick up yesterday afternoon for a romantic weekend and forgot to call because I've been more worried about you than what the hell day it is. So now I have to track her down to explain myself so she doesn't think I'm a world-class dick who disappeared on her because she's somehow not worth it. Because she's worth every fucking thing."

Ty's mouth had unhinged somewhere in the midst of this speech, and it occurred to Harrison that maybe he'd said too much. But damn it, he was exhausted and desperate.

"I'll get the laptop."

Ty came back a minute later and set the computer on the kitchen table. "So...uh, why is it you're having to look her up by computer and not just calling her?"

"Because I don't have her number."

"Why is that?"

As the computer booted up, Harrison told him the short version.

"Shit, you left all that for me?" Ty dropped heavily into a chair. "I'm sorry I fucked things up for you."

Harrison fixed him with a glare. "First off, you didn't fuck anything up. I did by not taking care of my own shit before leaving town. Second, don't you for a moment think I regret being here for you. You matter. Being here to help you when you're going through hell matters. Got it?"

After a brief hesitation, he nodded and dragged his chair around so he could see the screen. "So how are you going to track her down?"

"She's an author, so I figured I'd look her up on social media.

She's bound to be on Twitter or Facebook, or maybe her email address is on her website."

Harrison typed *Blake Iverson* into the Google search bar.

"Wait, Blake Iverson is a chick?"

"It's a pseudonym. And yeah."

"Damn. Didn't expect that. Love her books."

Her website was the first thing to pop up. He clicked on it, noting the slick design highlighting *Hollow Point Ridge*. There was a page listing her books, another linking to her fan forum. He clicked on that, wondering if she'd been active since she got home. The current membership was listed at 96,428.

"Holy shit, that's a lot of fans," Ty muttered.

"No kidding."

There was a ton of activity on the forum, but none of it appeared to be from Ivy herself. A little more clicking took him to a contact page that linked to all her social media profiles. He didn't actually follow her anywhere, so he wouldn't be able to send a direct message unless she accepted a friend request. And given what she probably thought of him right now, why would she do that? The contact page didn't list a specific email address, but it had a contact form. He clicked in the box and then paused.

"What's the problem?" Ty asked. "Don't know what to say? I figure 'I'm sorry' would be a good start."

"No, it's not that. Or not entirely. She's a big freaking deal. What if she doesn't handle all her own social media and stuff? She might have an assistant for that, and I don't want to get filtered out as being a nut job or something. Plus...this is really something that should probably be explained in person."

"So what are you gonna do?"

A popup appeared on the screen.

First ever public appearance! Meet the reclusive Blake Iverson and get your copy of Hollow Point Ridge *autographed by the author. Bonus: Get the special inside track on her brand new series. Parthenon Books, Nashville, Tennessee.*

"She's having a book signing in two weeks," Harrison murmured. "She never does public appearances." What had her agent and editor had to hold over her head to get her to agree to that?

"Great, so you know where she's going to be and when. So you can show up to plead your case in front of a couple hundred strangers."

It wasn't ideal, but this was his shot. He was going to put himself out there and risk rejection. It was part of that whole "choosing life" thing they'd talked about. But it wasn't really about choosing life. It was about choosing her.

He could only hope that she'd decide to choose him back.

hy the hell did I agree to this?

Nerves danced a jig in Ivy's belly at the sight of all the people packed into Parthenon Books. A banner hung at the front proclaiming "First Ever Appearance of Blake Iverson, Author of Best-Selling Sloan Maddox Series."

Her publisher had agreed to the expanded production timeline, but in exchange they'd wanted to do something to wow the public and rev them up. With her new protagonist being a woman, Wally had strongly pressed for Ivy to break her streak of no public appearances and let the world know she was a woman. So she'd agreed to this signing and an extremely limited tour after the book was published.

She was already regretting it.

In the center of the store, rows of folding chairs were set in front of a podium. Every one was filled and the crowd standing at the fringes was three deep. Each person she saw held one of her books in their hands, mostly the latest one, *Hollow Point Ridge*. The sight made her queasy.

"Can I have your attention please." At the podium, Peter, the bookstore manager, cleared his throat. As the crowd quieted, he smiled. "Thank you. Today is a momentous day, not only for Parthenon Books, but for publishing in general. We have with us the notoriously reclusive author of the Sloan Maddox series for her first-ever public appearance."

At the "her" a murmur ran through the crowd. The mutant butterflies in Ivy's stomach grew five sizes.

"She is a six-time *New York Times* best-selling author and the winner of numerous awards, and she's chosen us do a special reveal of her brand-new series, coming out this fall. Please give a warm, Nashville welcome to Blake Iverson." He led the applause as Ivy stepped from between two aisles of books and took the podium.

She curved her manicured fingers around the edge and looked out over the audience without really seeing them.

I will not faint. I will not faint. Blake Freaking Iverson does not faint.

Ivy sucked in a breath and tried for a smile. "Good afternoon. So, I imagine I am a bit of a surprise. My publisher has been very careful over the past few years to hide the fact that I'm a woman. But with the launch of this upcoming series, which features an absolutely kickass female protagonist, we felt it was a good time to come forward. You can consider yourselves part of the inner circle now." A faint wave of laughter rippled through the assembly.

"I'm not much one for public speaking, so how about we just get straight to the reading?"

With a deep breath, she smoothed her hands over the printed pages of the first chapter and began to read.

"*To my grumpy lumberjack, thanks for both rescues.*" She didn't know why she'd started with the dedication. She didn't know why she'd dedicated it to Harrison, except that, regardless of how things had ended, she wouldn't have finished the book without him.

"This is *Enemy of Silence.*"

Her voice wobbled at first, but gained strength with every word as she lost herself in Annika's story. By the end, the store was so silent, she could've heard a pin drop. Ivy didn't dare lift her head.

Oh God. Oh God, they hate it. They hate me. They—

The silence was eclipsed by thunderous applause.

The band around her chest loosened and suddenly she could breathe again. Heat flushed her cheeks as she waited for the noise to die down again. The worst was nearly over.

"We'll do a little Q and A before I move over to the signing table." She fixed her gaze on a middle-aged man in glasses. "Yes, you in the second row?"

"What made you decide to write a woman as a protagonist for this follow-up series?"

"I didn't start out with Annika, actually. My editor was pushing hard for Michael, but the book just wasn't gelling. At least not for him alone. Then someone suggested that he could be made that much more compelling if he was paired with someone who could make him peel back his armor. I realized that was absolutely true. It was Annika's story I really wanted to tell. She was interesting and compelling, and I wanted to know more about her past and how it was going to inform her present. I wrote the first draft of the book in a week."

Her gaze shifted to a thirty-something woman standing at the edge. "Yes?"

"So are you saying this particular book has more of a romance thread than your previous work? Are you planning on branching out into romantic suspense?"

Ivy considered the question. She'd loved that aspect of the story, and Wally wanted to play it up in revisions. But going back to that, after the disappointment of things in Eden's Ridge, was more pain than she was ready to cope with. She couldn't imagine chasing that on a regular basis. "As an author, I've learned never to say never. I don't presently have aspirations of shifting to romantic suspense, but I do intend to explore the relationship between Annika and Michael over the next several books. Their history is complex and interesting, and watching them overcome it will make for some pretty compelling fiction."

Someone spoke up from the back, "Who's the lumberjack in the dedication?"

Ivy froze. It couldn't be. "I'm sorry, could you repeat the question?"

The crowd shifted and there he was. Harrison Wilkes, in all his big, badass Ranger glory, dressed up in a sport coat and tie. "Who were you referring to in the dedication?"

Her breath clogged as her heart leapt into her throat. Relief and joy that he'd come, that he'd found her, had her knees going weak. Then reality crashed in. He'd walked away without a word. So what the hell was he doing here now?

Realizing her silence had gone on too long, Ivy swallowed. "He's someone I thought I knew better than I did."

The rest of the Q and A passed in a blur. Once Peter called the questions to a close, Ivy thought she'd be able to sneak away for just a few minutes to say, "Hey, how are you? And oh hey, you wanna tell me why you ran away from me?" but Peter herded her toward the signing table like a border collie with a recalcitrant sheep. She lost sight of Harrison.

Please don't leave.

Stupid. Leaving was apparently what he did best. The intensity of her bitterness surprised her. She thought she'd put that behind her, but she'd really just shoved it under the sofa cushion. She remembered what she'd said to him at the cabin weeks ago.

"Some hurts can be packed away and forgotten about, and they'll fade with time. And some become caged animals that do more damage, become more feral, the longer they're ignored."

Evidently her issues with Harrison fell into the latter category.

The line of fans snaked through the store, seemingly endless. The author in her was giddy that so many people had turned out to support her and the new series. The woman wanted nothing more than for all of them to go away so she could satisfy the curiosity that had nagged her for the past two weeks. What that would look like, Ivy had no idea. In an ideal world—or a romance novel—they'd run toward each other in the crowded store, and he'd sweep her into his arms for a passionate kiss that put the ones from last month to shame. Preferably with a swell of orchestral strings in the background.

She was not in an ideal world. She was in one of the city's top, independent bookstores for her first public appearance, with what felt like half the city wanting a moment or five of her time. So she did her job, smiling and chatting with readers, signing their books, thanking them for coming. Peter kept a fresh bottle of water at her elbow and a bouquet of her favorite pens. And the readers kept coming.

When familiar, rough hands thrust a copy of *Hollow Point Ridge* in front of her, Ivy almost didn't want to look up.

"Grumpy lumberjack, huh?" The rumble of his voice sounded above her.

Ivy's chest constricted with a bitter mix of longing and fury. He'd *left* her. Why should she still want him? Why should the sound of his voice make her ache with the desire for him to circle the table, haul her out of the chair, and pull her into his arms?

Because she knew without a doubt that if he did, once those strong arms anchored her against his hardness, his warmth, she'd be home. For all her years moving from place to place, she'd never felt so adrift and dissatisfied as she had since she came back to Nashville. Nothing made it go away. But he could. If he'd just close that last bit of distance between them, put his arms around her and draw her close, she'd be able to breathe again.

Except she wouldn't. Because the whole notion that he was home, that they'd actually built something between them had been pure artistic fantasy on her part. Not something real. Whatever she'd felt happening between them had been entirely on her side. It had to have been because he'd just walked away without a word. And after she'd spent the last two weeks struggling to put that behind her, to reclaim some sense of normalcy, he had the damned *nerve* to show up here and make her feel all this stuff again.

Shoving all that down deep to deal with later, Ivy lifted her gaze to his.

God, he looked good. His dark hair was streaked from the sun and he'd shaved for real this time. No more hiding? Looking into those eyes she'd dreamed of so often, Ivy still felt the spark.

But what the hell did sparks matter? Attraction hadn't been their problem. He'd still walked away.

"Not so grumpy underneath it all. And not so lumberjack, either. You clean up well, Harrison."

The sport coat only accentuated his broad shoulders. His shirt collar was unbuttoned, and the tie he'd worn earlier was stuffed into a pocket.

"Less of a place for flannel and a mountain man beard in the real world."

"What is your real world?" It was a question that had haunted her these past weeks. One of many she'd kicked herself for not asking.

"That's something I need to talk to you about."

Now? He chose *now* to want to talk? Ivy gestured to the line behind him that snaked all through the store. "I'm kind of in the middle of something."

"That's fine. I'll wait."

Opening his book to the dedication page, she muttered "Yeah, I've heard that before," and scrawled an inscription. Forcing a smile, she handed the book over. "Thanks for reading."

They stayed linked by the book for long seconds before Peter cleared his throat again and hurried Harrison along. Ivy watched as he wove through the crowd and sat in one of the cushy chairs scattered throughout the store. They'd see what kind of patience he had.

The line seemed to multiply every time Ivy looked up. But she did her job, smiled her smile, made conversation, signed books until her hand cramped, even as she made herself a promise to never do this again. By the time it was over, hours later, she expected Harrison to be long gone. But he was still perched in his chair, reading.

It was foolish to feel hope at that. He was probably just here to say hi.

He didn't just wait two more hours to say hi.

So maybe he was here to clear the air. Or something. Just because he'd waited didn't mean he wanted anything more.

She thanked Peter profusely for all the hard work he and his staff had put into making the signing a raging success. And then she was finally free.

Bracing herself, she crossed over to the man she couldn't forget.

You owe me ten questions, but I only have one. Why?

If he'd needed any further evidence that he'd hurt her, this was it.

Waiting for today had been hell. Being away from her had been hard enough without knowing she thought he was an asshole. Having to sit, day after day, while she concocted who knew what false explanations for his absence, always casting him as the bad guy because he'd hurt her, was intolerable. And he knew exactly how good she was at concocting villains. Getting here today, seeing her again—it had taken every shred of control he had not to just grab her up in the middle of everything and start babbling, "I'm sorry."

Over the past two weeks, he'd considered and rejected more

than a dozen grand gestures, wanting to make it clear to her in no uncertain terms how he felt. Those always went over well in the movies. But given how much she already hated public speaking and the fact that she'd looked about ready to jump out of her skin at all the people packed into the bookstore, drawing even more attention to her seemed like a bad idea. It was one thing to know that Ivy was a big freaking deal. It was a whole other to actually see it. The sheer number of people who'd turned out for the signing was overwhelming and had him wishing for their cabin in the woods, and the focus wasn't even on him.

So he'd waited, trying to read the book he'd had her sign and being entirely unable to focus.

To my grumpy lumberjack, thanks for both rescues.

He chewed on that. No matter what she thought, no matter how pissed and hurt she was, surely she wouldn't have dedicated the book to him if she didn't feel *something* for him.

"Sorry that took so long."

At the sound of her cool voice, Harrison's heart kicked into high gear. He rose to his feet, taking in her stiff posture and the wary look in those pretty, silver-green eyes. Everything he'd planned to say spilled out of his head. "Christ, it's good to see you."

Ivy's brows furrowed at that. "Forgive me for not really believing that, Harrison."

The sound of his name on her lips, even in that irritated tone, thrummed something deep in his chest. That helped him get started.

"I deserve that. But it's not what you think."

She crossed her arms, looking unimpressed. "Really? You didn't just totally ghost on me?"

"No. At least not on purpose. It was a life-or-death situation."

"A life-or-death situation. Because we have a lot of those as writers. Or are you even really a writer? Because I couldn't find your stuff."

Jesus, had he told her so little? "Nothing I ever said to you was a lie. I use a pen name, same as you. John Patrick Russell."

A reluctant curiosity stole over her face. "Why?"

He sucked in a slow breath to brace himself. This hadn't been on his list of things to talk about today. "John Laraway, Patrick Conroy, Russell Jennings. They're the men I lost. It was...a small way to honor them."

Ivy's expression softened. "I'm sorry."

Harrison just shook his head. "No, stop. I'm here to apologize to you. Not for leaving, because I had to go, but for the fact that I didn't manage to get a message to you first, to let you know what was going on."

"And that was?"

"One of my best friends tried to commit suicide."

All the color drained out of her face and so did whatever fight she had. "Oh God. Is he..."

"He's okay. Now. Or, at least, he's working to be. There were several of us on rotation for a suicide watch. I have the most flexibility of schedule, so I took the lion's share. And I just...lost track of days. By the time I realized I'd missed picking you up, you'd already left for home."

She closed her eyes, shook her head. "God. I'm so sorry."

"It wasn't your fault. What are you apologizing for?"

"For all the awful things I thought. I thought you'd ghosted me. I thought the whole damned week had been a lie and that everything between us was—" She cut herself off, as if she'd said too much.

But it was enough. It was maybe everything.

He stepped into her as he'd wanted, curving his hands around her shoulders and drawing her in so she looked up at him with glimmering eyes. "Nothing about that week was a lie. It was maybe the most real and honest I've been with myself and anybody else in years. So I hope you believe the unvarnished truth when I tell you that I'm completely and utterly crazy about you.

Not because you're a distraction or were convenient or any other craziness you might have convinced yourself of the last few weeks. Because you see me. You see straight into the scarred, battered heart of me. And maybe it's not the greatest package in the world, but it's yours—I'm yours—if you want me."

His heart beat thick in his throat as he waited for a response. He couldn't read anything on her face beyond total stupefaction. Beneath his hands, she trembled, and he wanted to draw her in, wrap his arms around her until she softened against him. But he needed something, some sign that they were on the same page with this.

"Harrison." Her voice was choked and a tear leaked out to trail down one cheek.

Shit, he'd made her cry. Were those good tears? Tears of regret because she'd realized she didn't want this with him?

"There is nothing in this world I want more."

He barely had time to register the relief and joy before she was dragging him down by his lapels and he was pulling her to her toes, and he didn't know who had started it but his mouth was on hers and—oh God—he'd missed this, missed her. As the chaos of his emotions swirled around him, he tightened his hold because she was his anchor. She opened for him and the taste of her flooded his senses, washing over every raw nerve and soothing. She was every bit as sweet as he remembered, and he needed so much more than just this taste in the middle of a busy bookstore.

Apparently coming to the same conclusion, she broke the kiss, easing back far enough to look into his face. "Give me your phone."

It wasn't what he'd been expecting. "What?"

She dropped back to her feet. "Your phone. Give it to me."

As his brain slowly came back online, he pulled it out of his pocket and handed it over. Her fingers lingered over his as she took it, even though he still had one hand around her waist, holding her firmly against him.

Her fingers flew furiously. "We aren't doing this again. This is every stinking number I have and my email address, and I just texted myself so I have your number." She gave it back. "I'm not taking any chances on losing you again."

This was the Ivy he knew, the one he'd fallen for, who could find the humor to ease over the rough patches. "What about your address?"

"That, too. Although I'm not trusting GPS navigation. I'm taking you there myself. Now, if you don't have anywhere else to be."

Lips curving into a grin, Harrison cupped her face. "There is nowhere I'd rather be than home with you. There's so much I want to tell you."

On a sigh, Ivy pressed her cheek into his hand, the last of the tension draining out of her. "Home."

As he looked into her smiling eyes, he was pretty sure he'd found his.

EPILOGUE

*J*vy set down the obscenely heavy box with a gasp. "Remind me again why we thought moving the week after finishing a book tour was a good idea."

Harrison set down two identical boxes labeled *Books* in the opposite corner of the room that would become her office. "I believe there was some plan for hitting up the spa once we actually got everything off the truck. Also something about wanting to get as far away from cities as fast as humanly possible because you couldn't with all the people anymore."

"Okay, yeah, I did say that." She'd known she'd be stressed to the max after the book tour launching *Enemy of Silence*, so going more or less straight to their new mountain hideaway had been the obvious choice when choosing a closing date for the house. She'd had visions of unpacking fast, then luxuriating in the quiet. But she'd underestimated the chaos of combining households and moving four hours away from Nashville. "But where the hell did all this stuff come from? I swear, it multiplied like tribbles in the truck."

"Perhaps a better question is how it is we all ended up being your manual labor? You could totally have sprung for movers, Miss Seven-Time *New York Times* Best Seller," Sebastian griped.

Ivy blew him a wink and a kiss. "But then I wouldn't get to see your pretty face." In the nine months since she and Harrison officially got together, she'd gotten to know his friends well and enjoyed razzing them at every opportunity.

"Besides, you're getting beer and pizza," Harrison reminded him. "What more does a man need?"

"I'm not sure there's enough beer in the Ridge to make up for all these boxes of books," Porter groused. "How many are there?"

"Forty. Ish," Ivy admitted. Maybe closer to fifty, but who was counting?

"Who the hell needs forty boxes of books?" Ty asked, adding two more to the stack.

"Two cohabitating writers." When he just sent her a flat stare, she hunched her shoulders. "What? Don't look at me like that. They're research."

"I'm looking at you like that because I'm pretty sure the entire forty-ish are all yours."

She looked to Harrison for some backup but he just crossed those massive arms and grinned. "He's not wrong. Almost all mine are digital."

On a huff, she folded her own aching arms. "I'm a writer. Therefore, I do not have a book problem."

"Would the same apply if you were a liquor store owner with half the contents of the store in your house?" Sebastian asked.

"Books are not a controlled substance."

"Maybe they should be." He easily evaded the throw pillow she snatched up from the loveseat.

"Troglodyte!"

His laughter echoed all the way down the hall.

Shaking her head with a reluctant smile, Ivy flopped down on the loveseat, glancing around at the three full walls of built-in bookcases and imagining them filled with colorful spines. It would be glorious. Perhaps not quite on the scale of the *Beauty and the Beast* library she'd lusted after since she was a child, but it would be hers. Theirs. Part of the home they'd chosen to build together.

The other half of that home joined her on the loveseat, tugging her in close. "We're nearly done."

Ivy eyed the mountains of stuff. "Your definition of done and mine are vastly different."

"Well, the truck's nearly empty, meaning we can feed and water the help and kick them out, the better to christen our new house."

With a hum of anticipation, she snuggled in. "We should establish an incentive for unpacking."

"Like a naked incentive? Miss Blake, I do like the way you think." He leaned in to kiss her.

"Hey, the last boxes on the truck aren't going to move themselves." Sebastian let the ones he carried land with a *thud* on the pile next to the loveseat and shot them a meaningful look.

Harrison cheerfully flipped him off and took Ivy's mouth in a smacking kiss.

"Get a room."

"We bought several, thanks."

Sebastian shot his own middle finger over one shoulder on his way out of the room.

Ivy watched him go. "We really need to get him a woman."

"Pretty sure Deanna would volunteer for that position. She was eying him pretty hard while we were loading the truck."

"She's absolutely in a Look-Don't-Touch phase, and definitely not into the idea of long-distance."

"Her loss. But they'd probably kill each other anyway." Harrison hefted himself up. "We'd best get back to it."

"I'll be along in a minute." Ivy slipped her phone from her pocket and opened up the browser, refreshing the page she'd been checking all day.

"Are you looking at the *USA Today* Best-Seller list again?"

"Maybe."

"I don't know why you keep doing that. My book is not gonna be on it."

In the months since Stormamageddon, he'd finished up the quartet about Coop's military service and begun a new series about life away from war, as a peacekeeper out on one of the far-flung frontier planets. Their release dates had been only a week apart, and Ivy simply couldn't get over how hands-off he'd been. Once he'd published the book, let his mailing list know, he was done, mentally moving on to the next book as he traveled with her on the two-week book tour her publisher had arranged. But after he'd been outed as the grumpy lumberjack in her dedication and dragged on stage for one of the morning shows she'd been interviewed on—to the absolute delight of the audience—Ivy had gotten an idea.

The page loaded and she began to scroll. "You never know."

And there it was. Number ninety-seven. *The Remains of Yesterday.* Ivy shrieked and began to dance. "I was *right!* See? *See?*"

She shoved the phone in his face.

Brows drawn together, he took the phone from her hand and stared, his expression slowly morphing into shock. "I don't...*How?*"

She bit her lip. "I might have shared the video from our clip on *The Breakfast Club* with my fans and totally pimped the book. And put together a Facebook ad campaign for the launch."

At the time, she'd felt delightfully sneaky, hoping she'd be able to surprise him. But now, she couldn't read his reaction. Would he feel like the success wasn't really his? That hadn't occurred to her until right this moment when he wasn't jumping around and celebrating as she thought he should.

Lowering the phone, he stared into her eyes. "Why?"

She resisted the urge to knit her hands. "Because you deserve it. The book's amazing. All I did was tell people the honest truth about that. Because I believe in you."

He slid his hands into her hair, tipping her face up so she couldn't look away. "I love you. I love that you'd do this for me."

She waited, the tension in her belly drawing tighter. "But?"

"No buts. No qualifiers. I just love you. Thank you." He brushed his lips over hers once, twice. A sweet gesture that had her melting against him in relief.

"I love you, too. And you're very welcome."

Sebastian's voice cut in on the moment. "If you two are done playing kissy face, the only thing left on the truck is this ridonculous bed you bought. It's gonna take all four of us to move it."

Harrison let her go with a grin. "Priorities."

As the love of her life headed back outside, Ivy couldn't help but think how life was strange. Strange and absolutely perfect.

∽

Choose Your Next Romance

You know we're getting another of this band of brothers, right? Next to fall is Sebastian. His match is a power house of a woman who's going to challenge everything he thinks he wants. Fans of my Misfit Inn quartet will love *What I Like About You* one for the Reynolds cameos, Athena and Logan's wedding, and, of course, Ari.

If you haven't yet checked out The Misfit Inn, it begins with *When You Got A Good Thing*, Sheriff Xander Kincaid's story. This whole series is all about the family you make and the bonds between sisters.

Can't decide? Keep turning the pages for a sneak peek of both!

WHAT I LIKE ABOUT YOU

RESCUE MY HEART #2

A horse-whispering loner

After years as an Army Ranger, Sebastian Donnelly is content to be left alone with his horses. He's better with them than with...people. But that changes when his boss's little sister shows up. There's something about her, a vulnerability that tugs at his need to rescue. And a sexy, vivacious charm that ignites an attraction he ought to ignore.

A soon-to-be lawyer

Desperate for a break before her last semester of law school, Laurel Maxwell is excited to see her brother marry the woman he loves. Logan and Athena, their happiness, the life they're building at the farm all serve as a reminder that she's barreling toward a future she's no longer sure she wants. One her overbearing father insists is the only path she's meant for.

Who's rescuing who?

When Laurel is offered the chance to stay on the farm and dogsit while the happy couple honeymoons, she jumps at the chance to get out her life and into Sebastian's strong arms. He wants to help her make her decision, a choice with haunting echoes of his own past. But is there any path that leads to a forever where a brilliant lawyer and reclusive horse trainer could build a life together?

~

CHAPTER ONE

Sebastian Donnelly shifted in the saddle, giving the chestnut mare a subtle nudge with his knee. After only a moment's hesitation, Gingersnap switched directions, resuming her trot around the training ring.

"There's a girl."

Her ears swiveled back toward the sound of his crooning voice, so he kept up a low patter of one-sided conversation as they continued to circle. She was attentive to every touch, every signal, every shift of his weight, and it was immensely satisfying that she did it out of a desire to please him rather than out of fear.

She'd come a long way in the eight months since she'd been rescued. No one looking at her now would know she'd spent the last few years of her life subjected to profound neglect and abuse. She'd put on weight, so her ribs no longer showed through. The coat that had been dull and matted on her arrival now shone with a gleam. The mane and tail he'd spent weeks detangling, as he slowly, methodically earned her trust, fluttered with the breeze of her movement. He'd waited months before going near her with a saddle and bridle, and longer still before trying to ride her. She hadn't been ready. But over the past few weeks, it had become clear that she'd had training before landing with the asshole who'd let her damn near starve to death. The sweet temperament he'd seen beneath the fear had emerged like daffodils in the spring, and Sebastian marveled that her spirit hadn't been fully broken.

This was the joy and the miracle of the work he did. The work that had saved his own broken spirit.

A flash of movement at the rail caused a hitch in Ginger's gait. Sebastian saw his stable girl climbing up so she could see better.

"She's looking fantastic!" At fifteen, Ari was bright, eager, and utterly besotted with all things equine. She'd been trading stable labor for additional riding lessons since the spring, so she was a familiar part of Sebastian's day.

"Coming along," he agreed, slowing the mare to a walk.

"Can I ride her?"

Sebastian shot her a look. All of his rescues had an assortment of behavioral issues he'd been working on since they came to the farm, and many weren't part of the group he used for lessons.

Ari folded her hands and put on her begging face. "Please? Just for a few minutes? I could stay on the lunge line."

He considered it. She'd proven herself a capable rider, quick to take instruction or correction, and Ginger was turning out to be a gentle, responsive mount. It might be a good fit.

Even as he thought it, the mare tensed beneath him and began to dance. Her ears twitched in agitation. Then he heard what she had.

Thunder.

It rolled over the land, echoing off the mountains that cupped this little pocket of paradise. As Ginger gave a little buck and twist, sidestepping across the ring, Sebastian ignored Ari, switching his full attention to his mount.

"Easy. Easy. Settle."

Tension crackled around her as he brought her in line. She quivered beneath him, nostrils flaring as he held her through another rumble of thunder. Her war between an instinct to flee and a desire to please him was evident in the way she tossed her head, eyes rolling. Storms were a huge trigger for her, and the only way to overcome that trigger was to keep pulling it, making her face it. Given their exceptionally dry autumn, there'd been limited opportunity to work on it, so he had to take the chances as they came.

For another twenty minutes, he battled her fear, taking the mare through her paces, despite the incoming storm. Ginger's anxiety was a palpable thing, and Sebastian deliberately banked his own emotions, knowing she'd ultimately mirror him. He just had to remind her of that trust. When she hesitated, he coaxed her through. When she danced, he reminded her to follow his lead. And when the first fat drops of rain began to splatter, he relented, reining her in long enough to dismount. Stepping close, he laid a hand on her quivering neck. "It's all right. You're all right."

Ginger held for him, though it was clear in every tense muscle that she still wanted to bolt. Stripping the saddle as quickly as possible, he heaved it over a rail and led her to the adjacent pasture. There, he removed the bridle and set her loose. As the next boom of thunder rolled, the mare took off at a run, kicking up her back legs and galloping a wide circle of the pasture as the other horses looked on. A few were already plodding toward the three-walled shelter to get out of the rain.

Ari came to join him, hood up and hands shoved into the pockets of her coat against the cold December wind. "Think she'll ever get over her fear of storms?"

"Maybe someday. She's got a long way to go." He didn't know what had happened to the mare to instill this abject panic, but he'd learned early on that keeping her in the barn was a non-starter. It was a damned miracle she hadn't broken a leg in her terror the one time he'd tried. All in all, the entire herd did better when they weren't confined.

Sebastian and Ari both stared after Ginger for another couple of minutes, waiting until she'd run off her first burst of anxiety. He couldn't stop the worry or the guilt the niggled. Had he done enough? Should she be further along? It was fruitless speculation. The mare was where she was. There were only so many hours in the day, and the reality was that many of his were tied up with the riding school. It was a necessary evil—one he hoped would eventually make his rescue program self-sustaining. But that was a long way off. For now, that meant more time with students and less time one-on-one with his rescues. Slower progress was still progress.

"Help you clean up?" Ari asked.

"Appreciate it." Sebastian hefted the saddle, while she grabbed the bridle, and they made their way to the barn. "You got a ride home?"

"Logan's taking me. Are you sure it's not a problem I won't be around for the next few days?"

Her earnestness amused him. "It's not every day your aunt gets married. It's fine. Logan's bringing in some extra help for dealing with the rest of the stock while he and Athena are away."

The man himself showed up as they were stowing gear in the tack room. "Looks like we're in for a gullywasher."

"Yep," Sebastian agreed. "Worst ought to be done before too late tonight, though."

Logan slung an arm around his soon-to-be niece. "You about finished, kiddo?"

"I need to grab my backpack from the house."

He jerked his head. "Go on and do that. I wanna try to get you home before the storm breaks."

When he continued to linger after Ari had run off, Sebastian knew he had something on his mind.

"Something up?"

"Well, I actually wanted to ask a favor."

"Is there something else you needed me to take care of, while you and Athena are gone on your honeymoon?"

"What? Oh, no. It's about the wedding itself. My college friend Nick is one of my groomsmen, and he's not gonna be able to make it. His dad just had a heart attack this morning."

"That's terrible." *What does that have to do with me?*

"Yeah. It's looking like he's gonna be okay, but Nick doesn't want to leave him, and anyway it puts us one man short on my side. I was hoping you'd be willing to be a stand-in groomsman."

Sebastian blinked. "You want me to be in your wedding?

Logan's mouth quirked up in a grin. "I know it's last minute and there's a monkey suit and all that. But I consider you a friend and it happens you're about Nick's build."

Sebastian wasn't exactly keen on getting up in the middle of all the wedding festivities. There was a reason he worked with horses instead of people. Still, he owed Logan a lot.

The man had taken on a handful of horses simply because there'd been a need and he'd had the space. With his hands already full from managing all the moving parts of his organic farm, he'd needed help. As a favor to their mutual friend, Porter, Logan had turned over the care of the horses to Sebastian, giving him a job, a home, and a new purpose—something that had been sorely lacking since he'd separated from the military. He'd fully supported Sebastian's expanded equine rescue efforts, going so far as to delegate a solid chunk of acreage and the original barn at Maxwell Farms to that purpose. Over the past eleven months, and through the joint labor of fully restoring that barn to be a working stable, he'd become a friend. He'd stood for Sebastian through some seriously dark days, and Sebastian was humbled to be asked to stand up with him on one of his brightest.

"I'd be honored, man."

He blew out a relieved breath. "You're saving my ass."

"Athena doesn't strike me as the type to give a shit whether the numbers are even or whatever." The award-winning chef would probably only care about the food, so long as they were married by the end of the day.

"She's not. My mama is. None of us want to deal with her fretting about what Emily Post etiquette thing isn't being met."

Clearly, Logan fell a very long way from that particular family tree.

"What do you need me to do?"

"The rehearsal is tomorrow at 4:30 up at the Methodist church. After that, we'll all be headed back to the inn for the rehearsal dinner. I'll see that you get the tux when you get there. Then it's just showing up at one on Saturday to do pictures before the ceremony and hanging out through the wedding and the reception after. Once the final group pictures are taken, you're free to bail."

"I'd planned to be at the wedding and reception anyway." He was a sucker for wedding cake, and rumor had it that Athena's pastry chef from her former Chicago restaurant was making it.

"Great. I really appreciate it, man." Logan offered his hand.

"No problem. Guess I'll be seeing you at 4:30 tomorrow."

As Logan headed up to the house to grab Ari and take her home, Sebastian rubbed a hand over his beard, noting it had gotten kind of scraggly. His horses didn't give a shit what he looked like, but he still had enough of his mama's voice in his head telling him what was right and proper. Looked like he'd need to clean up like civilized folks.

～

LAUREL WAS SO LATE.

She had reasonable faith that her big brother wouldn't excommunicate her from the wedding party and, from what she could tell, neither would his bride-to-be. But she knew perfectly well her mother would be having a hissy fit right about now, and nobody wanted to deal with that.

She'd been all set to get out the door of her Nashville apartment on time for the four-hour drive. But then The Call had come. The official job offer from Carson, Danvers, Herbert, and Pike up in New York. Roger Pike had called her himself to say how excited they all were to have her—as if it was a foregone conclusion that she'd accept the job, pending her upcoming graduation and the passing of the bar exam. It should have been.

Newly-minted attorneys were not supposed to turn down offers from a top-five firm in the nation. Especially one with a starting salary like the one Pike had thrown at her. It had taken all of Laurel's considerable skill with words to navigate the conversation without giving an actual answer. Then another loss of precious time to come down from the post-call spaz so she was safe to drive.

She'd already been wound up about seeing her parents this weekend without having the spectre of this job hanging over the proceedings. She couldn't tell them. Wouldn't, even if she'd accepted. This weekend was about Logan and Athena, not her latest effort to please her father. But with every mile into the mountains, her shoulders tightened and her stomach churned.

What if Pike had told Dad himself? They'd clerked together once upon a time, long before Laurel's father had opened his own firm. She didn't think the job had been a result of nepotism—her class ranking at Vanderbilt spoke for itself. But she knew connections mattered. And she knew if she said no, the shock waves would have far-reaching repercussions. So, priority one was keeping the news under wraps so Logan and Athena had a drama-free wedding. If Dad already knew about the offer—well, she'd find a way to talk him down so it didn't turn the weekend into a shit show.

In the end, she pulled into the lot of the First Methodist Church, in tiny Eden's Ridge, Tennessee, a whopping forty-five minutes late. Whipping her Mini Cooper into a space, Laurel took a few seconds to run a brush through her hair and thumb two antacids off the roll in her purse before sprinting in her sensible heels to the front doors. In the vestibule, she paused to bring her breathing under control. Rosalind Maxwell would consider gasping for breath an unseemly insult to Laurel's already unforgivable tardiness.

Beyond the double doors leading into the sanctuary, she could hear the murmur of voices. Crap, they were probably wrapping up already. It wasn't like it took that long to practice walking down the aisle. When she thought she could speak without wheezing—really, she needed to carve out time to get back into the gym next semester—Laurel stepped inside. The voices stopped and all eyes turned to her. She resisted the urge to hunch her shoulders, instead pausing in the doorway, spine straight, shoulders back, all her debutante training coming to her aid.

If you're going to make an entrance, make an entrance.

"I'm so sorry I'm late. There was a pile-up on the I-40 on my way out of town." The lie rolled easily off her tongue. Traffic accidents fell under the heading of excuses her parents would accept. She could see them twisted around in a pew up front. Ignoring the moue of disappointment pinching her mother's pretty face, Laurel deliberately blanked her expression and strode down the red-carpeted aisle toward the assembled wedding party.

Grinning, Logan broke free of his position at the altar, long legs eating up the last several feet, so he could wrap her in a solid hug. "Good to see you, Pip."

She didn't bother rolling her eyes at the old nickname—short for Pipsqueak. Even in her heels, her brother towered over her. Instead, she burrowed in for a long moment, absorbing his natural calm. "Back atcha, big brother."

Hooking his arm around her shoulders, he led her the rest of the way to the front. "Everybody, I want y'all to meet my sister, Laurel."

She gave a little wave. As Logan began introductions to the rest of the wedding party, she was aware of her parents' disapproving glares.

"—remember Athena, and these are her sisters, Maggie, Kennedy, and Pru. And this young lady with the sappy, romantic grin is Pru's daughter Ari. She likes to matchmake. Consider yourself warned."

Ari snorted. "Whatever. You're here, aren't you? That's a three-for-three success rate."

"I'm not sure you can claim credit for all of those," Kennedy pointed out.

The girl crossed her arms. "Who was it who gave you all a stern talking to when you were being idiots?"

Pru shot her daughter a look of affectionate reproof. "What she means is she's an incurably nosy and interfering romantic."

"I regret nothing," the teenager insisted.

Logan ruffled her hair. "Noted, Nosy. Moving on. This is our wedding planner, Cayla Black; my friend, Porter Ingram; and you remember Xander."

Did she ever. Her brother's former college roommate was still hot. He was also very married. To Kennedy, if she wasn't mistaken. They'd been high school sweethearts, once upon a time, and life had given them a second chance.

"Good to see you again, Xander. Congrats on your own nuptials."

He wrapped her a quick hug. "Thanks. You grew up."

"Yeah, that happens. I'm all set to become a productive member of society and everything."

"So I hear. Never pegged you for law school as a kid."

Laurel's face felt stiff as she forced it into a smile. "It takes all kinds."

Logan continued with the introductions. "And this is Pru's husband, Flynn."

Flynn nodded with an expression every bit as impish as his daughter's. "A pleasure, to be sure." The greeting fell off his tongue with an unmistakable Irish brogue.

"This here is Master of Carbs, Athena's pal, Moses Lindsey. Moses is the genius behind our cake."

"I'm pretty sure that makes you the most popular guy at the wedding," Laurel told him.

His teeth flashed white against the burnished bronze of his face. "I aim to please."

"Please tell me there's chocolate." She folded her hands in supplication.

Moses jerked his head in Ari's direction. "Tiny over there already put in her order. There will be chocolate," he confirmed.

Laurel mimed a small fist pump. "You are a god among men." Chocolate cake would go a long way toward making up for the stress she'd endured this semester.

"And last but certainly not least, your escort, Sebastian Donnelly."

Laurel turned to the last groomsman and felt the faux, flirty smile slide right off her face. She froze there, hand partly outstretched as her gaze locked with a pair of deep, brown eyes. Her breath backed up in her lungs, and her heart slowed to a crawl.

His thick, dark hair was nearly black and just a little mussed, as if he'd combed it with his fingers straight from the shower. Broad shoulders tapered to a narrow waist and long, long legs. His button-down shirt clung to his arms in a way that told her he had plenty of muscle under the Oxford cloth, and she'd bet money there was a solid six-pack under there, too.

He stepped forward, taking her hand in his. "Hi."

As his long, callused fingers closed around hers, she could breathe again. A stillness seemed to flow out of him and into her, and all the running and the stressing and the anxiety that was her constant companion went quiet. Her breath came out on some-thing very close to a sigh, the tension in her shoulders leeching out. In its absence, the pulse that had turned sluggish began to gallop. All the prospective polite banter evaporated from her brain, leaving her with only one thought: *Holy shit, you're gorgeous.*

She couldn't very well say that, though.

Words. I need words. I'm supposed to be good at those. Casting around for something to say, she blurted, "What happened to Nick?" Goofy, bespectacled Nick, who used to give her noogies and didn't leave her a tongue-tied mess of attraction.

"His dad had a heart attack, so Sebastian is standing-in," Logan explained.

"Is his dad okay?" The question came automatically. Thank God, she sounded normal at least.

"Yeah, he came through surgery and woke up a few hours ago."

"Good," she murmured.

Sebastian still had her hand, still hadn't looked away. Why hadn't he moved? Why hadn't she? It seemed as if heat built between their palms, and Laurel wanted to bask in it.

She wasn't broken. After the last couple of years, she'd begun to think that Devon had been right. The last guy she'd tried dating, back in her first year of law school, he'd accused her of being a robot. She was driven and focused. In the grand scheme of trying to maintain her position at the top of her class through that brutal, first year of academic hazing, dating and sex hadn't been a priority. She hadn't been interested in anyone since. But standing here, palm-to-palm, with Sebastian Donnelly, she felt that interest roar to life like a furnace re-stoked. Heat rolled over her, and she could only pray she wasn't blushing.

One corner of his mouth quirked, as if he knew her brain wasn't firing on all cylinders. Christ, how was it legal for a man to have lips that sensual? The contrast to the neat, close-cropped beard did something to her long-dormant lady parts, and she couldn't help wondering what that beard would feel like on the sensitive skin of her inner thighs.

"—done with introductions, how about we do one last run through, so Laurel is up-to-speed, then we'll break for the rehearsal dinner. Okay?"

Jerking her attention to Cayla, Laurel pulled her hand free, resisting the urge to tuck it under her arm to savor the tingles from where he'd touched it. Her cheeks bloomed with warmth.

Good God, when was the last time she'd felt an attraction like this?

Pretty sure that would be never, she thought as she followed the other bridesmaids to the vestibule.

With half an ear, Laurel listened to the wedding planner reel off instructions. The rest of her was still back in the sanctuary, reliving the touch of Sebastian's hand. It wasn't the heat that drew her—though that had rocked her back plenty—it was the stillness. The same kind of calmness her brother had always exuded but... more, somehow. Rare and precious, that feeling called her more effectively than any siren. Taking her place in the line-up to walk down the aisle, she wondered what she had to do to get another hit.

Grab your copy of *What I Like About You* today!

WHEN YOU GOT A GOOD THING

THE MISFIT INN, BOOK #1

*I*n the mood for more Eden's Ridge? Check out Sheriff Xander Kincaid's story!

Charming, poignant, and sexy, *When You Got a Good Thing* **pulled me in with its sweet charm and deft storytelling, and didn't let go until the very last page. It has everything I love in a small-town romance!** **~USA Today Best-Selling Author Tawna Fenske**

She thought she could never go home again. Kennedy Reynolds has spent the past decade traveling the world as a free spirit. She never looks back at the past, the place, or the love she left behind —until her adopted mother's unexpected death forces her home to Eden's Ridge, Tennessee.

Deputy Xander Kincaid has never forgotten his first love. He's spent ten long years waiting for the chance to make up for one bone-headed mistake that sent her running. Now that she's finally home, he wants to give her so much more than just an apology.

Kennedy finds an unexpected ally in Xander, as she struggles to mend fences with her sisters and to care for the foster child her mother left behind. Falling back into his arms is beyond tempting, but accepting his support is dangerous. He can never know the truth about why she really left. Will Kennedy be able to bury the past and carve out her place in the Ridge, or will her secret destroy her second chance?

GET your copy of *When You Got A Good Thing* today!

ABOUT KAIT

Kait is a Mississippi native, who often swears like a sailor, calls everyone sugar, honey, or darlin', and can wield a bless your heart like a saber or a Snuggie, depending on requirements.

You can find more information on this RITA ® Award-winning author and her books on her website http:// kaitnolan.com. While you're there, sign up for her newsletter so you don't miss out on news about new releases!

CPSIA information can be obtained
at www.ICGtesting.com
Printed in the USA
LVHW081628220722
724184LV00014B/991